"They told me you used to be pretty fast," Kenny said.

"I got by."

"Least they could have done was give you a decent gun."

"It'll do."

Kenny studied Cherry a little longer, then holstered his gun.

"After fifteen years I figure the least you deserve is a chance."

"Don't do it, son."

"Do what?"

"Give me a chance."

"Why not?" Kenny asked.

Cherry grinned tightly and said, " 'Cause I'll kill you."

Also in THE GUNSMITH series

- MACKLIN'S WOMEN
- THE CHINESE GUNMEN
- THE WOMAN HUNT
- THE GUNS OF ABILENE
- THREE GUNS FOR GLORY
- LEADTOWN
- THE LONGHORN WAR
- QUANAH'S REVENGE
- HEAVYWEIGHT GUN
- NEW ORLEANS FIRE
- ONE-HANDED GUN
- THE CANADIAN PAYROLL
- DRAW TO AN INSIDE DEATH
- DEAD MAN'S HAND
- BANDIT GOLD
- BUCKSKINS AND SIX-GUNS
- SILVER WAR
- HIGH NOON AT LANCASTER
- BANDIDO BLOOD
- THE DODGE CITY GANG
- SASQUATCH HUNT
- BULLETS AND BALLOTS
- THE RIVERBOAT GANG
- KILLER GRIZZLY
- NORTH OF THE BORDER
- EAGLE'S GAP
- CHINATOWN HELL
- THE PANHANDLE SEARCH
- WILDCAT ROUND-UP
- THE PONDEROSA WAR
- TROUBLE RIDES A FAST HORSE
- DYNAMITE JUSTICE
- THE POSSE
- NIGHT OF THE GILA
- THE BOUNTY WOMEN
- BLACK PEARL SALOON
- GUNDOWN IN PARADISE
- KING OF THE BORDER
- THE EL PASO SALT WAR
- THE TEN PINES KILLER
- HELL WITH A PISTOL
- THE WYOMING CATTLE KILL
- THE GOLDEN HORSEMAN
- THE SCARLET GUN
- NAVAHO DEVIL
- WILD BILL'S GHOST
- THE MINER'S SHOWDOWN
- ARCHER'S REVENGE
- SHOWDOWN IN RATON
- WHEN LEGENDS MEET
- DESERT HELL
- THE DIAMOND GUN
- DENVER DUO
- HELL ON WHEELS
- THE LEGEND MAKER
- WALKING DEAD MAN
- CROSSFIRE MOUNTAIN
- THE DEADLY HEALER
- THE TRAIL DRIVE WAR
- GERONIMO'S TRAIL
- THE COMSTOCK GOLD FRAUD
- BOOMTOWN KILLER
- TEXAS TRACKDOWN
- THE FAST DRAW LEAGUE
- SHOWDOWN IN RIO MALO
- OUTLAW TRAIL
- HOMESTEADER GUNS
- FIVE CARD DEATH
- TRAILDRIVE TO MONTANA
- TRIAL BY FIRE
- THE OLD WHISTLER GANG
- DAUGHTER OF GOLD
- APACHE GOLD
- PLAINS MURDER
- DEADLY MEMORIES
- THE NEVADA TIMBER WAR
- NEW MEXICO SHOWDOWN
- BARBED WIRE AND BULLETS
- DEATH EXPRESS
- WHEN LEGENDS DIE
- SIX-GUN JUSTICE
- THE MUSTANG HUNTERS

TEXAS RANSOM

J. R. ROBERTS

JOVE BOOKS, NEW YORK

THE GUNSMITH #83: TEXAS RANSOM

A Jove Book / published by arrangement with
the author

PRINTING HISTORY
Jove edition / November 1988

All rights reserved.
Copyright © 1988 by Robert J. Randisi.
This book may not be reproduced in whole or in part,
by mimeograph or any other means, without permission.
For information address: The Berkley Publishing Group,
200 Madison Avenue, New York, New York 10016.

ISBN: 0-515-09809-4

Jove Books are published by The Berkley Publishing Group,
200 Madison Avenue, New York, New York 10016.
The name "JOVE" and the "J" logo
are trademarks belonging to Jove Publications, Inc.

PRINTED IN THE UNITED STATES OF AMERICA

10 9 8 7 6 5 4 3 2 1

PROLOGUE
I
Outside of Huntsville Prison, Texas
June 1

Will Cherry walked out of Huntsville Prison with a great sense of relief.

Cherry had spent the last fifteen Junes in Huntsville Prison. There had been times over the past fifteen years when he really thought he'd never get out alive, never have his chance for revenge. There were a few times when he thought it might be better for him to die than go on living in prison, but then he'd remember how he came to be there, and he'd go on living, fueled by hate and a desire for revenge.

Now he was out, all legal and square. He'd paid his debt to society, and now he was a free man.

Free to kill the man who had put him there.

Sam Rogers.

II
Geneva, Texas
May 24

Sam Rogers looked at the calender on this desk. It was May 24. In a week it would be fifteen years to the day that Will Cherry had gone to Huntsville Prison.

On June 1, he would get out.

Sam could put himself in Cherry's place and know what Will Cherry would want to do first.

He'd want to kill Sam Rogers.

In fifteen years Sam Rogers had come a long way. He was a far cry from the drifter he was then. Now he was a respected, wealthy Texas rancher, with a town that he had built himself. Geneva, Texas, had been built as a shrine to his late wife, and named after her. He didn't want his past to touch it.

There was a knock on his door and he took his eyes away from the calendar.

"Come in."

The door opened and his foreman, Joe Bowman, entered.

"Mr. Rogers."

"Joe, come on in. Shut the door."

Bowman closed the door behind him and approached his boss's desk.

"Joe, I understand you know . . . that you're acquainted with . . . with a man named Kenny."

Bowman frowned.

"Gil Kenny?"

"Yes, that's him."

"Kenny's a gunman, Mr. Rogers. He doesn't hire on as a ranch hand."

"I don't want to hire him as a ranch hand, Joe." Bowman frowned again.

"Is something brewin' that I should know about, Mr. Rogers?"

"No, Joe," Rogers told the younger man. "No, this is personal. Could you put me in touch with him?"

"Well, sure, but—"

"Please, Joe. Do this for me and then . . . forget that I asked."

Joe Bowman regarded his employer for a few moments, then leaned on his desk and said, "All right, Mr. Rogers, but I want you to know . . . if you need my help for *any* reason, all you have to do is ask."

Rogers smiled at Joe Bowman.

"I know that, Joe. Thanks."

Bowman nodded, then left.

Sam Rogers sat back. It had been years since he'd even talked to a man like Gil Kenny. Now he was going to hire him.

To kill Will Cherry.

III
Outside of Huntsville Prison, Texas
June 1

Will Cherry wanted to get as far from Huntsville Prison as he could. He was given exactly what he'd had when he was locked up: clothes, a gun, and a horse. The clothes were old—if not fifteen years old, then damned near it. The gun was near as old, and the horse was near dead.

Cherry mounted the horse and rode for a mile before he stopped to check the gun. It would fire, but he was going to have to get himself a new weapon as soon as possible.

He was about to continue when he heard a sound behind him.

"Don't move," a voice said.

Cherry froze.

The voice behind him chuckled now.

"After fifteen years I guess your ears ain't what they used to be, huh?"

"I know you?" Cherry asked, trying unsuccessfully to place the voice.

"Nah, you don't know me, friend."

"What's this about?"

"Death."

"Mind if I turn around and see it comin'?"

There was a long pause, and then the voice said good-naturedly, "Hell, no. Turn and look—keep your right hand away from your body, though."

Cherry turned the horse with his left hand on the reins, his gun hand held away from him.

The man holding a gun on him was about thirty-five, a good sixteen years or so younger than Cherry. He was dressed in trail clothes, but even covered with dust, Cherry could see that they were fairly expensive duds.

"You followed me from Huntsville?"

"That's right."

"Gunman?" Cherry asked.

"Right again."

"For hire?"

"You're good at this."

"Sam Rogers?"

The man hesitated, then said, "I don't reveal the name of my clients."

"Clients?" Will Cherry said, laughing. "Is that what they call them these days?"

Cherry could see that the man was studying him with interest. He either knew him, or had been told about him.

"What's your name?"

"Kenny, Gil Kenny."

Cherry nodded.

"You heard of me?"

"Sure," Cherry lied. "Even inside."

"They told me you used to be pretty fast," Kenny said.

"I got by."

"Least they could have done was give you a decent gun."

"It'll do."

Kenny studied Cherry a little longer, then holstered his gun.

"After fifteen years I figure the least you deserve is a chance."

"Don't do it, son."

"Do what?"

"Give me a chance."

"Why not?" Kenny asked.

Cherry grinned tightly and said, " 'Cause I'll kill you."

Gil Kenny frowned, and then suddenly it dawned

on him that he might have made a mistake. He went for his gun again, but it was too late. He could see it coming.

Cherry drew and fired. The bullet hit Kenny in the forehead. It jerked him from his saddle and blew away the back of his head. When he hit the ground it was with a wet, slapping sound.

Cherry dismounted and went over to examine the man. The way he'd fallen there wasn't any blood on his shirt and, if Cherry acted fast enough, there wouldn't be.

The dead man was a little thinner than Cherry, but roughly the same height. Cherry stripped the dead man, then himself, and then donned the dead man's clothing. As he had expected, it was expensive stuff. The shirt was a bit tight across the shoulders, but the pants were all right. The boots were maybe a size too big, but they were better than what he'd been wearing. He checked the pockets and found better than two hundred dollars, some of it in silver.

He removed his own gun belt and dropped it to the ground, then removed the dead man's. The gun was a .45, some model that Cherry had never seen before, but it was a pretty gun, also expensive.

As he strapped the gun on, he figured that Gil Kenny had probably been fairly successful at what he did. He probably charged a lot, too.

That meant that Sam Rogers had money—and a lot of it.

That made it even better.

Maybe he wouldn't have to kill good ol' Sam.

Not right away, anyway.

He picked up the dead man's Stetson and put it on,

then mounted his roan. The horse was young and strong, and the saddle was black, hand-tooled leather. Cherry would get his own clothes soon, but he'd keep the gun and saddle, and probably the horse.

Ready to ride on, now considerably better outfitted than he had been moments before, he looked down at the dead man and said, "I'd thank you, son, but the man I ought to thank is Sam Rogers, because he sent you to me. And I'm gonna do that little thing . . . in person."

IV
Geneva, Texas
June 15

Sam Rogers was sitting at his desk when the knock came at the door. He looked up from the ledger he'd been unable to concentrate on and called out, "Come in."

Joe Bowman opened the door and came in.

"Any word?" Rogers asked. It had been two weeks since Gil Kenny had gone after Will Cherry.

"I'm afraid so, Mr. Rogers," Bowman said.

"Cherry?"

"He's alive."

"And Kenny?"

"Dead. They found his body about a mile from the prison. He'd been stripped."

"Was Kenny any good?"

"To tell you the truth, Mr. Rogers," Bowman said,

"he was a good hand with a gun, but he wasn't all that smart."

"Cherry's still good, then," Rogers said. "All those years behind bars, and he's still good."

"Mr. Rogers," Bowman said. "I could get Will Cherry for you. Fact is, before you gave me this job I made my way with a gun."

"No, Bowman," Rogers said. "I'm not going to send you after Cherry."

"Mr. Rogers—"

"He'll be coming here for me," Rogers continued, "and I'll need you here."

"Are you sure he'll come?"

"Oh, he'll come, all right."

"How can you be sure?"

"Because I would," Rogers said, "and once upon a time, Will Cherry and I were a lot alike."

"Not anymore."

"Maybe not," Rogers said, "but if I had spent fifteen years in prison, I know how I'd feel. He'll come, all right. He'll come. . . ."

V
Goldwood, Texas
July 1

Nina Engel worked on Will Cherry's rigid penis with obvious pleasure. She had never run across a man his age who could stay hard for so long, and then come back soon after being spent. In fact, she'd never met *any* man who had his staying power.

Nina was twenty-five and had been with a lot of men. She prided herself on her staying power, but she had to admit she was hard put to stay with Will Cherry.

He was honest, too. He told her that he had been in prison for fifteen years. To her he looked solid and strong, but according to him he still had to put on twenty pounds to be as physically strong as he had been when he went to prison.

"Twenty pounds," he'd said, "and fifteen years."

"Are all men who get out of prison . . . like you?" she'd asked breathlessly at that point.

"What do you mean?"

"I mean . . ." she'd said, encircling his cock with her hand, "so . . . so . . ." and she tightened her hand around him.

He'd laughed and said teasingly, "Honey, I'm the runt of the bunch!"

Now she was riding his penis with her mouth, marveling at how smooth and hard it was. The sides of him, wet with her saliva, were almost as slick as glass.

She was just about to have him pop for the third time when there was a knock at the door.

"Stop," he told her, pushing her away.

That was another thing she couldn't believe. As much as he obviously enjoyed sex, he was able to just tell her to stop and push her away when something else came up. Then, he'd go right back to her as if nothing had happened.

Well, she could wait.

It was worth it.

"Come in," Cherry called.

The door opened and Johnny Sangster entered. Sangster was about Nina's age, and Cherry had found—both in prison and out—that he had little patience with men that age. That was why he'd been pleasantly surprised to find Sangster. Cherry liked him. The younger man was a throwback to the days when Cherry was twenty-five. He listened, and he learned.

Sangster eyed the naked Nina for an appreciative moment, then switched his gaze to Cherry. Nina didn't bother to cover herself up. Cherry didn't like when she did that.

"You got something nobody's ever seen before?" he'd asked her the first time she'd done it, and it had made sense to her. From that point on she never covered herself when someone entered the room, and for that matter he never did, either.

"Everybody's here, Will."

"Dan Malone?" Cherry asked. "Frank Carter? Henry Wood? The Breed?"

Sangster nodded. "All of them."

Malone, Carter, and Wood were ties to Will Cherry's past. The rest of the men he needed he left to Sangster to gather, and most of them were Sangster's age or a little older—surely under thirty. But Cherry felt he needed some men his own age around.

As for the man known simply as the Breed, Cherry had heard about him in prison, and when he came up with his plan, he knew he'd need the Breed.

"Get them all in the saloon," Cherry said, getting off the bed and grabbing his pants. "I'll be there in just a few minutes."

"Sure, Will," Sangster said. He started to close the door, then stopped and said, "Will?"

"Yeah?"

Sangster stepped back into the room. "I think I

deserve to hear what's going on . . . you know, before the others?"

Cherry eyed the young man for a moment, then nodded and said, "Yeah, you're right, Johnny. You do. You know that fella I asked you to find out about?"

"Sam Rogers?"

"And the town he built?"

"Geneva, just about twenty miles south of here."

"That's right. Well, we're going to take that town, Johnny."

"We're gonna rob the bank?"

"No, Johnny," Will Cherry said. "Listen to me very carefully. We're going to take the town."

"The whole town?"

"The whole town."

Sangster digested that for a moment, then looked at Cherry and asked, "What are we gonna do with it?"

Will Cherry smiled and said, "We're going to hold it for ransom."

"The whole town?" Sangster asked again in disbelief.

"That's right, Johnny," Will Cherry said. "The whole town!"

ONE
Labyrinth, Texas
August 1

"It's almost too hot to make love," Loretta Jack complained.

"Too hot to make love?" Clint Adams asked.

She smiled at him and said, "I said 'almost.'"

Clint reached for her and pulled her across the bed to him. Loretta was a big girl, with large breasts and wide hips, and even as sweaty as she was, she was a pleasure to hold. Clint didn't mind sweaty women, not even in this heat. The scent Loretta was giving off only served to excite him more—a fact which she became immediately aware of.

"Jesus," she said, "you're so hard!"

"And sweaty," he said, reminding her.

"Mmm," she said, licking her lips and rolling her

eyes comically, "I don't mind at all."

To illustrate that point she bent her head and licked his belly, working her way down to his penis. When she reached it, she laved the head, then licked the length of it.

"Salty," she said, "and good."

She opened her mouth and took him deeply inside, and he gasped. Her head started bobbing up and down, her lips sliding along the length of him, and he reached for her head. She allowed him to show her the proper tempo, and then he released her head and laid back to enjoy the sensations that her mouth and teeth and tongue were causing.

When he was about to come, he reached for her and pulled her up next to him. He leaned over and began to lick her breasts and nipples, tasting the sharp saltiness of her and enjoying it. She moaned and reached for his head as his lips and teeth pulled on her nipples.

"Oooh," she said as his hand slid over her belly to her pubic mound. Deftly he slid one finger into her, and then a second as he continued to work on her breasts. She lifted her big buttocks off the bed in response to the manipulations of his fingers.

When he felt her shudder with the ghost of an orgasm he removed his hand, positioned himself over her, and then slid into her slowly, an inch at a time.

"Oh, yes," she breathed in his ear when his entire length was inside of her.

They began to move together, slowly at first, and then more quickly. Their wet flesh began to alternately make slapping and sucking noises as it came together and then parted.

He slid his hand beneath her to cup her buttocks

and take control of their tempo. As hot and sweaty as they were, he wanted to make this last as long as possible.

Loretta had other ideas, however.

She began to pull on him with her insides, demonstrating amazing muscular control for a waitress who refused to work as a saloon girl.

In moments they were both grunting and groaning, locked in a sort of combat which, seconds later, they both lost.

And won.

Afterward, Loretta went back to work at the cafe where she was a waitress, and Clint went to Rick's Place, his friend Rick Hartman's saloon.

T.C., the black bartender, drew him a cold beer as he approached the bar. The man's face gleamed with sweat, as did the huge biceps beneath his rolled-up sleeves, but as hot as it was, Clint never once heard the man complain.

"Got a lot hotter than this on the plantation," T.C. had told him once, and the subject never came up again.

Clint gratefully picked up the beer and drained half of it.

"Don't know how you can do it," T.C. said.

"What?"

"Tussle in the sheets in this weather."

"Depends on who you're tussling with."

"Loretta?"

Clint nodded.

"Rick tried to hire her, you know, but she wouldn't take the job."

"I guess she doesn't want to be a saloon girl."

"Rick treats his girls right," T.C. said. "Hell, you know that."

"I know. Where is Rick, by the way?"

"In his office. Friend of his came to town."

"Oh? Anybody I know?"

T.C. shrugged. "You know Sam Rogers?"

"The man who built Geneva?"

"That's the one."

"He's a friend of Rick's?"

"He knew Rick's pa."

"Rick's father?" Clint said. "Rick's never talked to me about his father!"

"Then don't expect me to."

"I don't."

Clint knew how loyal T.C. was to Rick, and would never have asked the black man any personal questions about Rick.

T.C. went down the bar to serve another afternoon customer who needed a cold beer to combat the heat. Clint finished his and was being given another by T.C., when the door to Rick's office opened and Rick stepped out in the company of a white-haired, prosperous-looking man. They shook hands, and then the older man left without looking at Clint or T.C.

"That Rogers?"

T.C. nodded.

Rick came over, and T.C. set him up with a beer.

"Where have you been?" Rick asked.

"Tussling in the sheets," Clint said.

"In this heat?"

"It depends on who you're tussling with," T.C. said.

"Who told you that?"

T.C. inclined his head toward Clint and said, "He did."

Rick looked at Clint and said, "Loretta?"

"Yep."

"I tried to hire that girl."

"I heard."

Rick sipped his beer and then said, "'I need a favor, Clint."

"Can't do it, Rick," Clint said.

"Can't do what?"

"Talk Loretta into working for you."

"I wasn't going to ask you that!"

"You weren't?"

"Hell, no. I got something much more important than that."

"Like what?"

"T.C., give the man a fresh beer. Can you come into my office for a while?" Rick asked Clint.

"Is it any cooler in there than it is in here?"

"No."

"Well," Clint said, picking up his fresh beer, "as long as the beer holds out."

TWO

"Sit down."

Rick sat behind his desk and Clint sat directly across from him.

"The man who just left was Sam Rogers. Do you know who he is?"

"I've heard of him."

"He was a friend of my father's."

Clint nodded and sipped his beer. Whatever it was Rick had to say, he'd tell it in his own time.

"He's got a problem."

"Like what?"

"Geneva—the town he built?"

Clint nodded to indicate that he knew about Geneva.

"Well, it's been taken."

"Wait a minute," Clint said. "What do you mean, it's been taken?"

"The town's been taken by a gang of men," Rick said. "It's being held."

"For what?"

"For ransom."

"Whoa, hold it a second."

Clint sat forward and rested his beer mug on Rick's desk.

"Who would hold an entire town for ransom?"

"A madman."

"I've never heard of this—"

"Will you just take my word for it?" Rick said testily. "It's being held."

"All right, all right," Clint said, sitting back. "I'll take your word for it."

"Well, don't," Rick said. "After we're finished here, I'm gonna check it out."

"You don't believe him?"

"I don't know—yes, I do, but—I don't know."

Rick seemed confused as well as annoyed, and Clint waited for it all to come out.

"Look, like I said, Rogers knew my father."

"A friend."

"What?"

"You said he was a friend of your father's."

"Yeah, I did say that."

Rick picked up his beer, and then put it down without sipping it. Instead he got up and went to a small sideboard, where he poured himself a brandy and downed it.

"I never liked Sam Rogers," Rick said, turning to face Clint, "but he was my father's friend."

"And now he needs a favor?"

"Right."

"And you feel obligated to grant it."

"Yes—if I can, that is. That's where you come in."

"Where I come in?" Clint asked. "Where do I come into this?"

"See, Sam knows that you and I are—that we know each other."

"Friends, Rick," Clint said. "The word is friends."

"Yeah, he knows we're friends." Rick went back to his desk and sat down. "See, he thinks you can do what no one else can."

"Which is?" Clint asked warily.

"He thinks you can go into Geneva and get him his town back."

Clint thought that over for a moment and then said, "Well, I'm glad *he* thinks so."

Rick came back into the office with a fresh beer for Clint and set it down on his desk. Then he went and sat behind his desk again.

"Well?"

"Well what?"

"Will you do it?"

"As a favor?"

"There's money in it, Clint," Rick said. "A lot of money, but I know how you feel about . . . hiring out, so I guess what I'm asking *is* a favor, yes."

"I'd need some men—"

"No."

"No, what?"

"Sam doesn't want the town shot up."

"Have they done any damage yet?"

"None. That's part of their threat."

"How much are they asking?"

Rick told him and Clint whistled.

"Can he afford it?"

"He has it," Rick said, "but paying it would break him. I guess that means he can't afford it."

"If he has the money and he wants to save the town, why doesn't he pay the ransom?"

"Because he thinks that once he pays, they'll destroy the town anyway."

"And kill the people?"

Rick hesitated.

"Rick?"

"He didn't mention the people," Rick said.

"Aren't they part of the town?"

"I guess. . . . He built that town to be a shrine to his wife, Geneva."

"I know that story," Clint said, "but the people are as much a part of the town as the buildings are . . . aren't they?"

"I guess. . . . I guess people can be replaced easier than buildings."

"So it's not that he's afraid that the people will be shot up, or killed, it's just the buildings?"

Rick shrugged helplessly and said, "I told you I never liked him."

"I wonder why your father did."

Rick looked away from Clint and said, "I . . . I never asked."

"So let me get this straight, then," Clint said. "Sam Rogers wants to hire me to go into the town—alone—and get it back from the men who are holding it. Is that it?"

"That's it."

Clint frowned, then said, "Uh, just how many men

are there holding this town?"

"He doesn't know for sure," Rick said evasively.

"Did he guess?"

"Yes."

"What was his guess."

"Twenty . . . or thirty."

"Twenty or thirty men are holding an entire town? And he wants me to get it back single-handedly?"

"I guess. . . . He's at the hotel. If you're interested you can get more information from him."

"Oh, I'd like more information, all right, like *why* someone would want to ransom his town."

"He didn't say."

"You didn't ask."

Rick shrugged.

"Same difference."

They sat in silence for a few moments, and then Clint stood up.

"Where are you going?"

"I'm going to talk to the man."

"Clint, I—"

Clint held his hand up to stop Rick from finishing what he was going to say.

"This is going to cost you, Rick."

"Sam has more money than—"

"Not money."

Rick frowned.

"What, then?"

"If I take this job, when it's all over I want you to talk to me."

"About what?"

"About your father and Sam Rogers."

Rick hesitated a moment and then said, "All right. I guess you'd deserve that—if you get it done."

"If I don't get it done," Clint said, "it won't matter, will it?"

"What do you mean?"

"I mean you could talk until you were blue in the face then," Clint said, "but I wouldn't be here to hear it, would I?"

THREE

Clint went over to the Labyrinth House Hotel and found Sam Rogers having lunch in the hotel dining room, alone.

One of the waiters, a man named Phil, saw Clint and started to come over, but Clint shook his head and headed for Rogers's table.

"Mr. Rogers?"

The man looked up, and it was obvious by the look on his face that he didn't know who Clint was.

"Yes?" he asked, his expression one of boredom.

"I'm Clint Adams."

If that fact thrilled Sam Rogers he hid it quite well.

"Sit down, Mr. Adams."

Clint sat and waited for Rogers to offer him something. He waited in vain.

"I assume you've talked to Rick?"

"I'll have some coffee."

"Excuse me?"

"Some coffee," Clint said, indicting the pot on the table.

"Oh, yes, of course."

Rogers motioned to the waiter, and Phil came over with another cup. He put it in front of Clint and poured the coffee for him, filling the cup to the rim. He knew that Clint drank it black.

"Thanks, Phil."

"Sure, Mr. Adams."

Phil left and Clint sipped his coffee.

"You've talked to Rick?"

"I have."

"He's told you what I want?"

"You want me to ride into a town full of armed men and get it back for you. Tell me something, Mr. Rogers, am I supposed to come out of this alive?"

Rogers frowned, showing displeasure at the way Clint was talking to him.

"It's not a prerequisite, Mr. Adams, but if it's at all possible, yes."

"Just as long as we know where we stand," Clint said.

"Will you do it?"

"I'll want some additional information first."

"Such as?"

"Why are these men holding your town?"

"It's not *my* town."

"You built it, didn't you?"

"Yes, but I do not own it."

"You have no say in local elections?"

"None."

Clint was surprised. It had been his experience that man like Sam Rogers liked to own things, especially if he was the one who built it.

"Do you own businesses there?"

"No."

Clint said nothing.

"Am I ruining your image of town bosses, Mr. Adams?"

"Obviously you are not a town boss, Mr. Rogers. I'm still working on what indeed you *are*, however."

"You seem like an educated man, Mr. Adams."

"I've never been to a university, if that's what you mean, but I've learned a few things over the years."

"You are not quite what I expected, either."

"Am I ruining your image of the hired gunman, Mr. Rogers?"

"Indeed you are."

"Who's the ramrod of this takeover?"

"I beg your pardon?"

Clint had changed the subject a little too quickly for Rogers.

"Who's in charge, who is it who is really holding the town?"

"A man named Will Cherry."

"Will Cherry!"

"You know him?"

"I know the name," Clint said. "About twelve or thirteen years ago he was a fairly well-known gun."

"Fifteen years ago," Rogers said. "He got out of Huntsville Prison on June first."

"What is Cherry to you?"

"Nothing," Rogers replied too quickly.

"Excuse me, Mr. Rogers, but you're a liar."

"What?"

"The man means nothing to you, and yet you know the exact date that he got out of jail? You'll understand if I find that hard to believe."

Rogers studied Clint for a few moments, then said, "Yes, I will understand."

"Good. What was your relationship with Will Cherry."

"We were partners . . . once."

"Fifteen years ago?"

Rogers nodded.

"What happened?"

"That really doesn't matter, does it? He went to jail and I went straight."

"And built Geneva."

"I built a life, I married a wonderful woman . . . and lost her. I built Geneva to honor her, and now Will Cherry is threatening to destroy it." Rogers paused for a moment, his eyes misting over.

"Mr. Adams," he said after a moment, "I would very much like you to save Geneva."

To Clint it sounded as if the man was talking about his wife.

Maybe he was.

"We'll leave in the morning, Mr. Rogers."

Rogers nodded, and Clint rose to leave.

"There is something else you should know," Rogers said before Clint could leave.

"What's that?"

Rogers hesitated before answering, "I already hired one gunman."

"Who?" Clint's eyes narrowed.

"Gil Kenny."

"Not bad. What happened to him?"

"Cherry killed him."

"Fair?"

"Near as we can figure."

"That wasn't smart."

"I know that," Rogers said. "I knew it when I did it."

"Are you afraid of Cherry, Mr. Rogers?"

"Oh, yes," Rogers replied without hesitation.

"All right," Clint said. "Thanks for telling me that."

Rogers nodded.

Clint started to leave again, only this time it was he who stopped.

"Mr. Rogers?"

"Yes."

"We should understand something."

"What?"

"If you refer to me as a gunman again, I'm out."

Rogers caught Clint's eyes and held them, then looked away.

"I understand."

FOUR

Clint went back to Rick's Place and found Rick leaning against the bar, talking to T.C.

"Jesus, that was fast," Rick said. "Did you see him already?"

"I saw him."

"And?"

"I don't like him, either."

"But are you going?"

"Yes," Clint said, "I'm going."

A knowing look came over Rick's face, as if he'd known all along that Clint would go.

"We'll be leaving in the morning," Clint said. "Can you get me some information before I leave?"

"On Rogers?"

"No," Clint said. "He's got too much money for that. He'll have hidden his trail well. No, I want you to get me some information on Will Cherry."

"Will Cherry?" Rick said. "I don't know the name."

"I do."

"What's he got to do with this?"

"He's the man holding the town."

"Oh. All right. You sure you don't want me to try and get you something on Rogers?"

"How much do you know about him?"

"Not much, really. Fact is, I hadn't seen him in five years until this morning."

"Get me what you can on Will Cherry," Clint said. "He just got out of Huntsville on June first, but I want before and after. Chances are you may run into Rogers along the way."

"All right."

"Oh, and Gil Kenny."

"Now there's a name I know. Is he one of Cherry's men?"

"No. According to Rogers, Kenny is dead, killed by Cherry."

"You want to know if he really is dead?"

"Right."

"When do you want this?"

"Tonight," Clint said. "If you can't get it by then, I'll need it at the crack of dawn."

"Yeah, sure," Rick said sarcastically. "I'll get it for you tonight."

"Fine. I'll be by for it."

"Where are you going now?"

"To have lunch."

"At the cafe?"

"Where else?"

As Clint walked out, T.C. looked at Rick and said, "Another tussle in the sheets."

"That sounds real good to me."

FIVE

Loretta had to work through the afternoon and into dinner, so any more "tussling in the sheets" that afternoon was out of the question. They agreed to meet at Clint's hotel later that evening. Clint had not yet told her that he was leaving.

When Clint walked into Rick's Place that night it was as mobbed as usual, being the most popular saloon of the four the town had. Rick was seated at a rear table with one of his girls on either side of him. The blonde woman on his left had the improbable name of Sheena, and was currently Rick's bed companion.

Clint approached the table, and all three of its occupants smiled at him. The redhead on Rick's right was named Jess, and she had been making eyes at Clint since she'd been hired four days earlier.

"All right, girls," Rick said. "Time to mingle."

Sheena leaned over and kissed him on the cheek, and as they left, Jess contrived to brush up against Clint with her round, solid breasts.

"Jess likes you." Rick said.

"Really. I hadn't noticed," Clint said, sitting opposite Rick with a beer he'd picked up at the bar. "What have you got for me?"

"What makes you assume that I *do* have something for you?"

"Because I know how badly you want to avoid getting up at the crack of dawn."

"Right," Rick said, sitting forward. "Will Cherry was a bad one before he went to prison, Clint."

"That much I figured out."

"I don't know what connection Sam Rogers had with him, though."

"You didn't come across Rogers's name?"

"Not at all."

"What did Cherry go to prison for?"

"Held up a bank and killed a man."

"Deliberately?"

"Apparently a stray shot killed a teller, but that didn't matter much at his trial."

"Did he get out June first?"

Rick nodded. "Just like you said."

"Like Sam Rogers said. What's he been doing since?"

"I don't know. He dropped out of sight."

"What about his friends?"

"After fifteen years?"

"Some friendships die hard. Who were his friends?"

"He was known to run with Dan Malone and Frank Carter."

"Those fellas all had their heydays."

"Like Cherry, they're all in their fifties now," Rick said.

Clint, who wasn't as far from fifty as he liked, said, "What's wrong with that? They ain't dead yet."

"Also Henry Wood."

"Hank Wood?"

"Yep, I thought that would catch your attention."

"I know Hank. We're not friends, but I know him. He was retired, had himself a ranch."

"Had is right," Rick said. "He lost it about a year back."

"What's he been doing?"

"Drifting, pulling jobs. He's wanted."

"Damn fool."

"That ain't all," Rick said. "He's riding with a character they call the Breed."

"Jesus," Clint said. "If Cherry's got Wood and the Breed, and the others with him, this isn't going to be easy."

"If you ride in there, is Hank Wood gonna remember you?" Rick asked with concern.

Clint rubbed his jaw as he thought about that. He hadn't seen Wood in almost ten years.

"That's an interesting question," Clint said. "Just to be on the safe side, I think I'll grow a beard."

"Well, you've got a pretty good head start there," Rick said.

Clint rubbed his jaw again, feeling the stubble there.

"So I haven't shaved in a couple of days. I'm not a well-dressed, dandified saloon owner."

"You could be," Rick said. "I've offered you a piece of this place often enough."

"No, thanks," Clint said, which was always his answer.

"Going to your hotel?"

"No," Clint said, "I've got a poker game lined up with a few fellas."

"Where?"

"Here," Clint said, indicating a table across the room, as far from the door and window as could be gotten.

"Still taking money from the poor merchants of this town, huh?"

"Unlike you, of course."

Actually, Rick offered very little in the way of gambling. What he did offer was good whiskey, cold beer, and the prettiest women in town—which was why he was after Loretta Jack to work there.

"Listen, you don't suppose before you leave you could put in a good word for me with Loretta."

"I have already."

"You have?"

"Sure."

"And?"

Clint grinned and said, "She didn't believe a word of it. She thinks all saloon owners are scum."

"You rushed to my defense and told her she was wrong, of course."

"Of course," Clint replied, "but like I said, she didn't believe a word of it."

In the next moment all joking fell by the wayside.

"I won't see you before you leave," Rick said.

"No."

"I want you to know . . . you can change your mind if you want to."

"No," Clint said. "Rogers is going to pay me a lot of money."

"If you come out alive."

"If I don't," Clint said, "it won't be any fault of yours, Rick."

"Just don't mess it up, Clint," Rick said, "so I won't have to deal with that question."

SIX

"Do you really have to go?" Loretta asked.

Clint leaned over and kissed her left nipple.

"It was time, anyway."

"Time for what?"

"For me to get moving. I can't stay in one place for very long, you know."

"When will you be back?"

"I don't know."

"Will you be back?"

"I don't know that, either."

She sighed and put her head on his chest.

"I guess a man with your reputation never knows if he'll be back or not."

"No."

"And I guess I have no way of knowing if I'll still be here if and when you do come back."

"I guess not."

She dipped her hand down beneath the sheet and said, "I guess that means that we should make this a night to remember."

"Yep," he said, lifting the sheet so she could slip underneath, "I guess . . ."

Her avid mouth began to work its magic on him and soon he was at a loss for words. All he could manage were moans and groans of pleasure as she milked him for every last drop . . .

Later, he turned her over onto all fours. As she stuck her gorgeous buttocks up into the air he slid his penis between her thighs and up into the wetness of her. He enjoyed the feel of her smooth cheeks nestled up against his belly for a moment, then started taking her in long, easy strokes. Every time he drove himself home she cried out loud, cursing him and praising him in the same breath. When she shuddered and came she grabbed ahold of the bedposts and almost screamed, and when he came his own cries almost raised the roof. . . .

Still later they made love in a more traditional position, but drove at each other so violently that the bed fairly walked across the room each time they came together. . . .

A couple of hours before daybreak Loretta woke Clint by crawling between his legs and using her tongue on his penis then sucking it until it was as hard as a railroad spike. He'd never run up against a woman with such a desire to use her mouth to drive a man crazy—and she did it so well. . . .

In the morning Clint left without waking Loretta. His legs were weak enough as it was, and he didn't think he'd be able to stand if he let her beneath the sheet one more time. The woman's mouth was as insatiable as it was lovely. . . .

He *had* brought up the subject of working for Rick Hartman—albeit only once—even though he had made no such promise to Rick. It was simply a fact that he felt Loretta would do better for herself working for Rick than as a waitress in the cafe. He had pitched it as a job where she would make more money, but she said the amount of money was not important. She wouldn't prostitute herself for any amount of money.

Clint had let the subject drop there. . . .

He had agreed with Sam Rogers that they would meet at the livery stable in the morning. Clint had arranged with the liveryman to have their horses saddled and waiting.

When Clint arrived at the livery he found Sam Rogers already there, giving Duke the once-over.

"This is a magnificent animal," Rogers said.

"Thanks."

"What is he, seven or eight?"

"Close to nine."

"Some men would prefer a younger animal," Rogers said, "but I can see why you prefer him."

"There's a lot to be said for experience, Mr.

Rogers," Clint said, mounting up.

Rogers mounted his Indian pony, which Clint looked over with appreciation.

"That's a fine-looking mustang," he said.

"The Indians know horseflesh," Rogers said. "Mustangs are small, but they can run all day."

The pony was young, and stood barely fourteen hands high but he exhibited the trademark strong legs; straight shoulders; short, strong back; full barrel, and intelligent eyes.

"It would be an interesting competition," Clint said.

"This is a fine horse," Rogers said, "but I wouldn't put him up against your gelding. I do, however, have a couple of animals on my ranch who might do the job. When this is all over, we might want to see about it."

Clint found the remark oddly comforting. It meant that Rogers had confidence that he'd get the job done.

He only wished he felt as confident himself.

SEVEN

Will Cherry found Johnny Sangster on the front porch of the Hotel Geneva.

"What are you looking at?" Cherry asked.

Sangster inclined his head across the street where Mayor Davis was standing with his daughter, whose name was Sonia. Sangster had found out that her friends called her Sunny, and that was what he'd started calling her.

"Oh, her," Cherry said. "Yeah, she's a young beauty, all right, but as cold as ice. You're wasting your time with her."

"Maybe," Sangster said, "but I didn't bring a woman with me, like some people."

"That was your oversight."

"Which I'm going to remedy."

Cherry slapped the younger man on the shoulder and said, "I wish you luck, but you'll have to get her away from her father, first."

"I'm working on it."

"How are things around town?"

"Quiet. When Breed broke that fella's arms it kind of convinced the others that resistance was futile."

"Well, that's fine," Cherry said. "I'm going over to the saloon."

"You'll find Hank Wood there."

"Drunk as usual, I assume."

"Yeah. He isn't doing us much good, Will."

"I know," Cherry said, "but he was a good man once, Johnny. Like Malone and Carter."

"They're fine. They don't get along with the others because they're older, but they get their jobs done and they take orders. I guess they know that taking orders from me is taking orders from you."

"I explained that to them and they understood it."

Sangster stood up, and Cherry saw that the mayor's daughter had walked away from him and was heading away on her own.

"Well, good luck, Johnny," Cherry said as Sangster stepped down into the street. "You're gonna need it," Cherry told the younger man's retreating back.

Cherry was glad he had brought Nina along. There wasn't a woman in town that appealed to him, and the pretty ones he had seen were all the same age as the mayor's daughter, or less—all too young. Nina was half his age, but that was just about his limit.

He had left her up in his bed in the hotel, where they had taken the largest suite. He had to admit that

Sam Rogers knew how to build a town.

He headed for the saloon, concerned about Hank Wood. He and Hank had pulled many jobs together twenty years ago, but the man seemed little more than a town drunk these days.

Well, as long as he didn't get in the way. . . .

"Sunny," Sangster called out, and the young girl turned in response to her name.

As he was every time he saw her, Sangster was taken aback by her beauty. She was about twenty, with long golden hair, full breasts, and an incredibly slim waist which served to make her bosom seem even fuller. She had blue eyes, large and liquid, and full, sweet-looking lips.

"Mr. Sangster," She greeted him stiffly.

"Hey, I thought we settled that," he said. "You're supposed to call me Johnny."

"You settled it," she said, "I didn't."

"Now come on, Sunny," he said, taking her by the shoulders. "You knew there was something between us the first time we met."

"Perhaps," she said, "but that was before you and your roughneck friends took over the town."

"What's that got to do with us?"

She pulled away from his touch and said, "There is no 'us' Sangster. There never will be."

"You're wrong," Sangster said, his tone taking on a menacing note. "One day soon there will be an 'us,' and you'll beg me for it."

"Not likely."

She started away but he grabbed her, pulled her to him, and tasted her lips for the first time. Even though she was resisting, he found the touch of her mouth heady.

"You're even sweeter than I imagined," he said, releasing her.

"I'd slap your face if I didn't think you'd take it out on someone else in town."

"I haven't hurt anyone."

"No, you let that half-breed friend of yours do your dirty work for you."

"It's not dirty work to him," Sangster said, grinning. "He enjoys it."

"So do you," she said, "only you're worse than he is. He likes hurting people, while you like watching it happen. I don't know who I should feel more sorry for, you or him."

"Don't feel sorry for me," Sangster said. "I'll have everything I want, very soon."

Somehow, Sunny Davis felt as if Sangster was talking about more than just having her. She shivered and walked away from the young man she had once thought she could be interested in.

Now the only interest she had in him was seeing him dead.

EIGHT

When Clint and Rogers arrived at Rogers's ranch, Clint couldn't help but be impressed with its size, particularly the house. It was one of the largest he'd ever seen.

"I built that house for my wife," Rogers said. "Now I live in it alone, with my daughter."

"Daughter?"

"Haven't I mentioned her?"

"No, you haven't." And neither had Rick, if he knew about her.

"Her name is Lynda, with a *y*. An affectation her mother insisted on. You'll be meeting her shortly."

They rode up to the front of the house where a man took charge of both horses.

"Treat that gelding with the respect he deserves, Layton," Rogers told the man.

"Yes, sir."

So far Rogers seemed to exhibit more concern toward his town and toward horses than he did for people. Clint wasn't sure he could ever like—or even respect—a man with that kind of attitude.

"Let's go inside," Rogers said.

Clint followed him up the steps and into a huge entry hall. A man in a dark suit approached and took Rogers's hat from him.

"Philip, this is Clint Adams," Rogers said. "Please show him to the best room in the house."

"Yes, sir."

"I have to go to my office and catch up, Mr. Adams," Rogers said. "You can have a bath, and I'll see you at dinner."

"I could use a bath," Clint said. "Thanks."

"We'll talk after dinner, and you can tell me what course of action you've decided to take."

"As soon as I come up with one," Clint said, "you'll be the first to know."

Clint followed Philip up to the second floor and down a long hall.

"This will be your room, sir," Philip said.

"Thank you, Philip."

"There is a bathtub inside. I will have it filled. Hot water or cold?"

"Hot, thank you."

"Can you tell me, sir, how long you will be using the room?"

"Probably just one night, Philip."

"Very well, sir. The water will be brought up shortly."

Clint nodded, and went inside. There was a huge four-poster bed with a thick mattress, a sofa, and a round table, as well as a dresser and some end tables. On the windows were heavy brocade curtains, in red.

"Too bad I won't be here for more than one night," Clint said, looking around.

Sam Rogers was in his office only twenty minutes when there was a knock at his door.

"Come in."

Joe Bowman entered.

"I heard you were back. He's with you?"

"Yes."

"I still say you don't need him."

"I know your views on this, Bowman. We've talked about it enough." Rogers's tone said he'd brook no further discussion about it.

"Yes, sir."

"You'll have dinner with us tonight."

"Yes, sir."

"Mr. Adams will have access to your help and to the help of any of our men. Is that understood?"

"Of course."

"Where is Lynda?"

"Out riding."

"Not alone!"

"No, sir. I have a man riding with her."

"Good. The town's been taken, the only other thing Cherry could take that means anything to me is Lynda."

"Maybe he doesn't know about her," Bowman said.

"He might not have originally, but he's been in town for a week. By now he knows."

"I suppose."

"All right," Rogers said, "I have some paperwork to catch up on. I'll see you at dinner."

Bowman recognized a dismissal when he heard it, and left the room.

He was looking forward to meeting Clint Adams, the legendary Gunsmith. He may not have agreed that they needed him, but meeting him was an opportunity not to be missed.

After Bowman left, Sam Rogers sat back in his chair and folded his hands over his stomach. He thought briefly of his wife's daughter, Lynda, his stepdaughter. He loved the girl as if she were his own, and he believed that she loved him. He'd married her mother when she was six and he was, after all, the only father she'd ever known. Now eighteen, she was as beautiful as her mother had been. In a few years she'd surpass her mother in that regard—as unbelievable as that seemed.

He rubbed his hands over his face. Whatever he said to the girl, he couldn't convince her of the danger she was in. Evidence of that was he fact that she was out riding, now, when he'd warned her not to leave the house.

Maybe he should have brought the Gunsmith here to protect her rather than to get the town free of Cherry's grasp. It was almost as impossible a task!

NINE

Drying off from his bath, Clint looked out the back window and saw that it looked down on the back of the house. As he watched, he saw a girl and a man ride into view and dismount. The girl was dark-haired and had a marvelous figure. He couldn't see her face, but from the way she moved he assumed that she was fairly young.

As he watched, the man took her by the upper arms, pulled her to him and kissed her. While they kissed his hands moved to her back, then roamed downward until each hand cupped a tight, round buttock. Abruptly, she pulled away from him, and when he reached for her again she slapped him hard on the face, then pranced away, laughing.

She walked toward the house while Clint looked after her and suddenly, as if she sensed his presence, she looked up at Clint's window and, for a moment, their eyes met. She was close enough to the house now for him to see that she was very young, and very pretty.

She disappeared from view then, and he assumed that she had entered the house through some back entrance. He moved away from the window and began to dress for dinner, wondering if he had just seen Lynda Rogers.

When he was dressed he studied his appearance in the mirror. His beard now colored the bottom portion of his face, although it was still more stubble than beard. Still, it did alter his appearance, maybe enough for someone he hadn't seen in nearly ten years not to recognize him.

Clint strapped on his gun and went downstairs to join his "employer" for dinner.

In her room Lynda Rogers undressed. She had run into her father as she came home, and he had of course scolded her for going out riding. She told him for the hundredth time that she could *not* be cooped up in the house or on the grounds all day..

Then her father told her that Clint Adams had arrived with him, and that she would meet him at dinner. In her room Lynda assumed that it had been Clint Adams who had been watching her from the window of one of the guest rooms. That meant that already Clint Adams knew more about her than her own father did. She had seen him fairly clearly in the window, and she liked the fact that he hadn't pulled back once their eyes had met.

Naked, she walked to the bathtub that Philip always had waiting for her when she returned from a ride. Before stepping in, she looked at herself in her wall-length mirror. As usual she liked what she saw—full, firm breasts, slightly pear-shaped with dark brown nipples; a slim waist; and flaring hips. She knew she had perfect thighs, although very few people other than herself and a few choice men had seen them, and she had shapely calves.

She settled down into the tub then, enjoying the feel of the hot water on her bare skin.

Lynda Rogers had lost her virginity to a ranch hand when she was fourteen, and had been sampling men very carefully since then. Of course, most of the men she'd had sex with over the past four years were ranch hands who, when she tired of them, she had always managed to have fired for one reason or another.

However, no man as yet had ever fully satisfied her—not the way her mother always told her a man should satisfy a woman. She knew, though, that she satisfied men very easily. She had learned how to do that over the span of four years and was very good at it.

As she soaped herself she thought about Clint Adams, whom her father had said was a legend in his own time—of which there were very few. Hickok was one, he had said, and Adams was another.

She stepped from the bath and dried herself slowly with a fluffy towel. She had not allowed Del, the man she had ridden with, to make love to her, although she had allowed him certain other liberties. The look on his face when she slapped him had been priceless.

She lingered over her breasts and nipples with the towel, then tossed it away and walked to her closet. She chose her dress very carefully. Her father would look at it and see his well-dressed daughter. Another man—like Joe Bowman, or even the Gunsmith—would look at her and have other thoughts entirely. She knew that the shade of green was perfect for her, because it brought out the green in her eyes—her mother's beautiful green eyes.

Before she dressed, she perfumed herself and thought about Joe Bowman. She knew that Bowman loved her, but so far she had only teased him. She knew that none of the other men who'd had her had told Bowman, because Bowman would surely have killed them.

Maybe she'd let him have her one of these days, but Bowman was too loyal to her father just now.

Perhaps she'd manage to turn his loyalty toward her one day. Maybe Joe Bowman—who ruled the ranch with an iron hand—would one day be the man to satisfy her.

When she was finished dressing, she studied the results of her efforts in the mirror.

She wondered how she would appeal to a legend?

And she wondered how a legend would appeal to her?

It would be interesting.

TEN

When Clint entered the dining room and saw the other man at the table, he knew that dinner wasn't going to be an entirely pleasant affair.

"Clint Adams, I'd like you to meet Joe Bowman, my foreman."

Clint was surprised. He had heard of Joe Bowman, and what he'd heard did not indicate that the man would make a good ranch foreman. Then again, he hadn't heard anything about Bowman for a couple of years now.

"Bowman," Clint said, extending his hand.

Bowman rose and shook Clint's hand, but there was no welcome in either the handshake or the eyes.

"I think I should make it clear that I don't think

we need you here, Adams," Bowman said.

"Bowman!"

"No, that's all right," Clint said. "I like things to be out in the clear. I've heard of you, Bowman, and from what I've heard you'd probably be a big help to me in this—if you're willing, that is."

Bowman opened his mouth to reply, then thought better of it and closed it. After a moment he spoke.

"I'll do whatever Mr. Rogers wants me to do, Adams."

"Well, that's fine, then," Clint said. "Maybe we'll get along."

"I don't think—" Bowman started to say, but he stopped short and looked past Clint.

Clint turned and saw Lynda Rogers, whose eyes met his boldly.

"Ah, Lynda," Sam Rogers said, approaching the girl. "Come and meet our guest." He guided his daughter to the table and said, "Lynda, I'd like you to meet Clint Adams. Mr. Adams is going to help us get Geneva free of the men who are holding it. Mr. Adams, my daughter, Lynda."

"Mr. Adams and I have already met," she said, studying Clint openly.

"Have you?" Rogers asked, puzzled.

"From the back window," Clint said. "I saw her ride in earlier."

"Ah, I see."

"Thank you for coming to help us, Mr. Adams," she said, extending her hand.

Clint took it and found her handshake very firm.

"I hope I can help, Miss Rogers."

"Please, call me Lynda."

"If you'll call me Clint."

"Hello, Lynda," Joe Bowman said. Clint had only to hear the hopeful tone in the man's voice to know that he was smitten with his boss's daughter.

"Hello, Joe," Lynda said, all but ignoring him beyond that.

As they seated themselves for dinner, Clint decided that Lynda Rogers was a very dangerous young lady. Very self-possessed—and possibly self-centered—she knew how to dress and what to say. He was sure that when Rogers looked at her he saw nothing more than a young girl he thought of as his daughter. She had dressed, however, so that other men would notice the full breasts, the green eyes, the dark tone of her skin.

Over dinner Lynda asked Clint, "Have you decided yet how you're going to get Geneva back?"

"Well, I—"

Rogers interrupted him. "Mr. Adams and I will discuss that later, my dear," he said, "in private."

Lynda laughed.

"You've just seen my father put me in my place, Clint," she said.

"Nonsense—" Sam Rogers said.

"My father puts everyone in their place, Clint. Has he put you in yours, yet?"

"Lynda—"

"Your father and I have established our relationship, Lynda."

"Oh, yes? And what is it based on?"

Clint looked her in the eyes and said, "Money."

She studied him for a long moment, and then said, "Oh, I doubt that. . . ."

As he had anticipated, the dinner conversation was

strained, more so for the fact that Lynda Rogers was ignoring Joe Bowman and giving Clint Adams all of her attention.

Bowman now had two reasons to dislike Clint.

After dinner Rogers rose and said, "If you'll excuse us, my dear, Clint and I will go to my office."

"Of course, Daddy," she said, turning her cheek for him to kiss. "Clint, make sure my father gives you the good brandy, the one from France."

"Thank you for the tip, Miss Rogers."

"Lynda."

"I'm sorry, I forgot . . . Lynda."

"Joe," Rogers said, "stay available. I'll want to talk to you shortly."

"Yes, sir."

"Adams!"

Rogers left the room and Clint followed.

"He's an interesting man, isn't he?" Lynda asked Bowman.

"Why are you asking me?" he said sullenly.

"You don't find him interesting, Joe?"

"You sure did, all through dinner."

"Why, Joe, are you jealous?"

"Hell . . . Lynda, why don't you marry me?"

"Because you're jealous, Joe," she said.

"That's because I love you."

"But you'd be so possessive," she said, shrugging. "I can't be possessed, Joe."

"A woman is supposed to be—"

"Not this woman, Joe," she said, standing up. "Don't forget that. I will never be any man's possession."

She turned and left the room, and Bowman looked

around for something to drink and found nothing but water.

He needed something stronger.

It occured to him then that he had never had any of Sam Rogers's French brandy.

Lynda Rogers rushed up to her room, annoyed with herself. When she got there she closed the door and leaned against it, her hand over her stomach, which had been doing flip-flops ever since she and Clint Adams had exchanged glances across the dining room.

It was a reaction for which she had been totally unprepared, and one that annoyed her to no end.

If she didn't do something about it very soon, it might get out of control, and Lynda Rogers had always prided herself on having control, of everything and everyone in her life.

This was not a threat that she could afford to let go unresolved.

ELEVEN

In his office Sam Rogers did indeed pour Clint Adams some of his imported brandy. He also offered him a cigar, which Clint refused.

"Let's get down to business, then," Rogers said, sitting behind his desk. "How do you intend to go about this?"

"Well, I've given the matter some thought," Clint said. "I think I'll ride into Geneva in the morning."

"That's it?" Rogers asked. "You're just going to ride in?"

"That's right."

"And do what?"

Clint shrugged. "Have to look around, do some scouting."

"Will you tell them who you are?"

"Not necessarily."

"What if someone recognizes you?"

"So what?" Clint said. "I'm who I am and I'm riding through town."

Rogers frowned and said, "I don't know about this. If you're recognized and Cherry suspects—"

"Cherry won't recognize me because we've never met," Clint said. "He's got some men with him named Malone and Carter, and they won't recognize me because I don't know them, either. I don't know his other men, but I'll have to take the chance."

Rogers looked at Clint in surprise.

"How do you know all of that?"

"I did some checking," Clint said, taking credit for Rick's work. Why not?

"I'm impressed."

Clint frowned and thought, what the hell.

"Don't be," Clint said. "Not with me. Rick got the information for me."

"I see."

"There is a man in there who might recognize me," Clint said, "but we haven't seen each other in nearly ten years."

"And if he does? Will you kill him?"

"No," Clint said, annoyed. "I wouldn't kill a man just for that."

"But if he tries to kill you—"

"That would be a different matter entirely, but even if Cherry and his men find out who I am, there's no reason to think they'll assume I'm working for you."

"You don't know Will Cherry," Rogers said, shaking his head. "He'll never assume you're there just by coincidence."

"And how well do you know Will Cherry after fifteen years?" Clint asked.

"Men like Cherry don't change."

"You changed."

"I was never like him," Rogers said vehemently. "I needed money, and it wasn't until later that I figured out there were other ways of getting it besides stealing it. He liked stealing, and he liked hurting people."

"Fifteen years in prison can do a lot to change a person."

Rogers shook his head.

"Not Will Cherry."

"We'll have to wait and see."

Clint sipped the brandy and then put it down on Rogers's desk, unfinished. He'd have preferred whiskey or a beer.

"I'll need Bowman."

"For what?"

"To be ready to ride in with some men in case I need them."

"Tell me what you want him to do."

"I think I'll tell him," Clint said. "It's bad enough that he resents me now. If I don't talk directly to him, it'll show a lack of respect on my part."

"You respect Bowman?"

"Do you know what Bowman did before he hired on with you?"

"He mentioned something about making his way with a gun. He was rather vague."

"Bowman was more than a decent hand with a gun," Clint said. "He vanished from sight a couple of years ago. Seems to me he's taken the right path."

"How good was he?"

Clint shrugged. "He was good, maybe even better

than good. The fact of the matter is, I respect what he accomplished, and I respect him even more for walking away from it before it got control of his life."

Rogers frowned and said, "Like it has with you, you mean?"

"We're not talking about me," Clint said quickly. "Could you get him in here?"

"Yes, of course."

Rogers left, and Bowman must have stayed extremely close by because they were back in moments.

Briefly, Clint explained to Bowman what he wanted from him, what he expected.

"Have you got some decent men working for you?"

"I've got a few good ones," Bowman said. "Enough to do the job."

"We don't have an accurate count of the men who are holding the town, and although I may get one once I'm in town, I may not be able to get it to you. You and your men can't just come riding in, you'll have to slip in."

"We'll be ready," Bowman said.

"I'm sure you will be," Clint said, standing up. "I want to get an early start in the morning, gentlemen, so I'll be turning in. Good-night."

He started for the door and then turned to face Rogers again.

"We should get one thing clear, Mr. Rogers."

"The money," Rogers said. "I'll be generous, Adams. If you want to set a price—"

"I'm sure you'll pay me what you think your town is worth," Clint said. "That's not my concern."

"What is, then?"

"I want you to know that I'm doing this for the people in that town," Clint said. "I will be more concerned for them than I will be for your buildings. Is that understood?"

"It is," Rogers said.

"Good-night, then," Clint said, and left.

After Clint left Bowman looked at Rogers and said, "Is that all?"

"Why didn't you tell me you had a reputation before you came to work for me?"

Bowman shrugged. "It never seemed important." Bowman didn't want to ask the next question, but he couldn't help himself. "Why, what did he say?"

"Just that he respected you for what you had done with your life, for someone who had started out making his way with a gun," Rogers said, using the same phrase Bowman himself had used. He still wasn't quite sure what "making his way" meant.

Bowman hoped that he had hidden his surprise—and pleasure—from Rogers.

"May I say good-night?"

"Yes, of course."

Bowman left Rogers's office. He was annoyed because of the pleasure it had brought him to know he was respected by the Gunsmith.

The man might just make it hard to dislike him.

Lynda Rogers was listening at her door for Clint Adams, and when she heard footsteps she closed the door and waited. Finally, she heard the door to the guest room close.

She'd give him a few minutes to get comfortable, but no more than that.

She couldn't wait much longer.

TWELVE

Clint had just managed to lie down on the bed when he heard somebody at his door. There was no knock, but someone was turning the knob—someone who obviously had a key. He heard the key slide into the lock, snick open, and then the knob turned fully and the door swung inward.

He leaped off the bed and rushed to the door and grabbed hold of the person coming through it. He pushed the person toward the bed, where they stumbled onto it, and then he was on her.

"Jesus, you're heavy," she said.

He looked down at the person he was lying on and saw that it was Lynda Rogers. He started to get off her but she put her arms around him and held him there.

"I'm not complaining," she said, and kissed him.

Her mouth tried to engulf his as she sucked first on his lower lip and then on his tongue. Clint became hard immediately, and Lynda wiggled her crotch against him.

"Lynda," he said, pulling his mouth away from hers, "this isn't a good idea."

"I disagree."

"Your father—"

"Doesn't have to know anything about it," she said, "but he will if you don't cooperate."

"What do you mean?"

"I'll scream," she said, smiling, "and I'll tell him that you tried to rape me."

"Would he believe that?"

"He believes anything I tell him."

He studied her for a moment, then said, "Yeah, I'll bet he does."

"Kiss me," she said, and he did, a perfunctory kiss on the lips.

"No," she said, "kiss me like you enjoy it."

He kissed her again, this time with fervor. The fact of the matter was she was an excellent kisser. She knew what to do with her nose, and her lips, and her tongue, and all the time her crotch was grinding against his.

"Mmm," she said, sliding her lips away from his, "you're a wonderful kisser. I knew you would be."

"Thank you."

"I have something to tell you."

"What?"

"I've been with a lot of men."

"No fooling?"

"I had my first man when I was fourteen, and a lot since then."

"To what do I owe the honor of this confession?" he asked.

"I've never felt the way I felt at dinner, sitting across from you. My heart was hammering, my stomach was nervous—"

"Maybe it was something you ate," he said.

"No," she said, her eyes shining, "but it soon will be."

She released him then and slid away from him. She was wearing something filmy that he was sure her father knew nothing about, and then it was on the floor.

"You're beautiful," he said, staring at her. He admired her pear-shaped breasts, and he knew they were firm because he had been lying on them.

He suddenly became aware of the fact that he was wearing only his underwear, because of the heat. If she had come in five minutes later she would have found him naked. His penis was pushing against the fabric, creating a tent-and-pole effect.

She moved close to him and went down to her knees. She freed his penis by sliding his shorts down to the floor, where he stepped out of them. Her cheek moved against his rigid penis, and then her tongue was tracing a wet line up the underside to the head, which she kissed juicily.

She opened her mouth then and took him fully into it. He put his hands on her shoulders and, at one point, was actually standing on his toes as she suckled him.

"Oh, God," she said, letting his penis free. It glistened with her saliva, and became very cool when the air hit it. "Oh, God," she said again, "let's get on the bed, please."

Since she had asked so nicely, he complied.

In bed she went wild.

When he entered her she gasped and clutched at him. She wrapped her thighs around him and drummed his buttocks with her heels. If he didn't know better he would have sworn that she'd just experienced her first orgasm.

Or maybe he didn't know better. . . .

"Jesus," she said breathlessly, "I've never felt anything like that!"

They talked for a moment and both discovered that in four years of having sex she had never before experienced an orgasm.

"You mean I've been wasting the past four years?" she asked him.

"I guess so," he said. "Maybe none of your, er, partners ever waited long enough for you to get your pleasure, as well."

"Uh, can it happen again?"

"Sure," he said. "Watch."

He kissed and sucked her breasts until her nipples were rock-hard; then worked his way down over her belly until his face was nestled between her legs. He licked her womanhood up and down, delved into her with his tongue, and then concentrated on her clitoris.

As soon as his tongue touched it, she shuddered and climaxed again, but he didn't stop there. He continued to work on her, holding her clitoris between his teeth and flicking at it with his tongue until she came again, more violently than before. He pinned her thighs down with his elbows so that she couldn't get away from him and continued to lick her until she started crying that she'd had enough.

"I don't believe this," she said, gasping as he lay down next to her.

"Believe it."

"Is it supposed to be like this every time?"

"If you have a good partner."

"Is it—can it be this good for you?"

"I always enjoy it," he said. "I enjoy giving pleassure almost as much as receiving it."

"If I offered you a lot of money, would you marry me?"

"No."

"What about just staying around for, oh, twenty years or so?"

"I'm sorry."

"What good is money if you can't buy what you want?" she asked.

"I wouldn't know. I never have all that much of it."

She rolled on top of him and kissed him.

"You can kick me out now. I won't scream rape."

"Oh," he said, palming her buttocks, "maybe in a little while . . ."

She put her nightie back on and then turned to face him.

"My God, I feel like I should thank you," she said.

"Don't."

"Are you sure you have to leave in the morning?"

"I have a job to do."

"How much is my father paying you?"

"I don't know."

"But I thought—"

"That I was doing it for the money?" he asked. She nodded and he shook his head. "I'm doing it as a favor for a friend, and I'm doing it to free those people."

"My father doesn't much care about people," she said.

"I noticed that."

"He's not really my father, you know," she said. "He married my mother when I was six."

"I see."

"I do love him, though," she said, "even if he is a bastard."

He didn't say anything to that.

Lynda walked to the bed, leaned over, and kissed him. He could feel the heat of her body, and feel himself responding to it. Still, they had agreed that it wouldn't be prudent for her to spend the night in his room.

"Make him pay you a lot," she whispered.

"I will," he said.

She walked to the door, then turned and said, "And make sure you're alive to collect."

He smiled and said, "I'm planning on it."

She peeked out the door to make sure no one was in the hall, and then she was gone.

Clint was lucky that he had turned in early, for after Lynda left his room he still had time to get some sleep. Still, after the nights he had spent with Loretta and Lynda, it was beginning to appear as if going into Geneva might be a safer course of action for him.

THIRTEEN

In the morning Clint had breakfast with Lynda, served by Philip.

"Where's your father" Clint asked.

"Probably out with Bowman. They both rise pretty early in the day."

"Necessary, I guess, if you're running a ranch."

"About last night—" she began.

"Last night was last night, Lynda," Clint said. "We both got something out of it, didn't we?"

"I hope so."

"We did," he assured her.

"I seem to have lost something also," she said.

"Oh? What?"

"My confidence," she said. "I've never had any problem dealing with men, but when I'm around you I . . . I don't seem to know what to do, what to say."

"I'm flattered—" Clint said, but he stopped when the front door of the house opened. Momentarily, Rogers came striding into the room.

"Are you ready?" he asked.

"Daddy, Clint hasn't finished his breakfast."

Rogers frowned, as if he'd just noticed his daughter's presence.

"What are you doing up this early?" he asked.

"Daddy—"

"You never get up this early."

"Daddy!" she said, looking at Clint in embarrassment. Obviously, she'd gotten up early to see Clint before he left, and hadn't wanted him to know that.

"Does Bowman have his men picked out?" Clint asked.

"Yes. They're outside."

"All right, I want to talk to them," Clint said, standing up.

"Clint," Lynda said, rising with him as her father left the room, "be careful in Geneva."

He smiled at her and said, "I'm always careful, Lynda."

She gave a quick look to see if her father was within range and then kissed him on the mouth.

"Be extra careful, this time."

"I'll see you soon."

She smiled widely and said, "I'm counting on it."

Clint left and found Rogers, Bowman, and five men waiting outside.

"Five?" he said to Bowman.

"The rest are just ranch hands," Bowman said. "Cowpunchers. These men know how to use a gun."

"Anybody here I'd know?"

"Cal Webster, over there on the end," Bowman said. "He's top hand, came here when I did."

Clint remembered the name. Webster was not a gunman, but he did hire his gun out for a while. Clint recalled that he was a reliable man.

"You wouldn't know the others."

Clint looked over the other four men and said, "They're young."

"So are most of the men that Cherry has with him."

Clint gave Bowman a quick look and said, "How do you know that?"

"I rode to a rise near town and gave it a look with a long glass," Bowman said. "I don't think he has more than three or four men over thirty."

Clint nodded and said, "It helps to know I'll be dealing with unseasoned stock."

"From both ends," Rogers said, as if he had just realized the import of that fact. "I could send for some help—"

"Save your money, Mr. Rogers," Clint said. "You're not going to get your town back by force . . . not in one piece, anyhow."

Clint stepped down off the steps and took a good look at the men. Two of them didn't even look twenty yet.

"How old are they?" he asked Bowman.

"They're all over twenty-one," Bowman said. "Bob Hansen, the one in the center, he's thirty. Webster is my age, thirty-four. We're the oldest."

"Have they been told what they'll have to do?"

"Yes."

"Have they been ordered to do it?"

Bowman looked at Rogers, who shrugged.

Clint faced the men and said, "What Bowman has told you—or will tell you—is that what we want you to do is risk your lives. You can't be ordered to do that. Anyone who wants out can withdraw now without being fired." Clint turned and said to Rogers, "Isn't that right, Mr. Rogers?"

"That's right, Mr. Adams."

"All right," Clint said, turning to face Bowman. "You know what to tell them."

"I know."

Clint approached Rogers, with Bowman next to him.

"I want each of these men to receive a bonus for risking their lives."

"How much?" Rogers asked.

"I'll leave that up to you," Clint said, and then added, "and Bowman." He looked at Bowman and asked, "Can I leave it up to you?"

"You can."

"All right," Clint said, "I'm going to saddle my horse and get going."

Bowman watched Clint walk to the stables. He was impressed that Clint was going to saddle his own horse when he could have told Bowman to have one of the men saddle it. He was also impressed about the demand for a bonus.

Yes, sir, this man could make it mighty hard to dislike him.

FOURTEEN

Will Cherry had Nina on all fours and was plowing her from behind. She was yelping in pleasure every time he slammed into her and was about to come when there was a knock on the door.

"Yeah?" Cherry shouted.

"It's me, Johnny."

"Come on in!"

Sangster walked in and stopped short when he saw Cherry and Nina on the bed. Cherry's penis was still buried deep inside of the woman, and she was on all fours with her head hanging down, breathing heavily.

"Will . . ." she bawled. "I'm close!"

"Take it easy, Nina," Cherry said. He stroked her

sweaty back, gentling her as he would a skittish pony. He looked at Sangster and said, "What is it, Johnny?"

"Hank Wood."

"What about him."

"He killed a whore last night."

"What?"

"Got stinkin' drunk, took a whore upstairs, and tried to wear her out."

"What happened?"

"Near as I could figure he couldn't get hard, so he beat her to death. She was found this morning by one of the other girls."

"Where'd they work? The whorehouse?"

"No, the saloon."

"Where's the sheriff?"

"Still in his office, with Stockwell."

"Cherry!" Nina wailed.

"All right, get out," Cherry said. "I'll be along directly. Wait for me at the saloon."

"Right."

Even before he left, Cherry began slamming into Nina again, and her high-pitched cry told Sangster that she'd gone right over the edge.

He left the room with a rock-hard erection, thinking about Sunny Davis and how she'd sound when she climaxed.

An half an hour later Will Cherry walked into the saloon, which had not yet opened for the day. Sangster was there with a couple of other men, including Dan Malone. Sitting at a corner table was Hank Wood, either still drunk or deadly hung over.

"Hank," Will Cherry said, "what the hell happened?"

Wood lifted his head off the table but didn't answer. Cherry stepped forward and backhanded the man across the face. Wood went crashing to the floor.

"Didn't I tell you that no one was to be killed?" Cherry shouted at him.

Wood looked up at Cherry, his mouth bloodied.

"I'm sorry, Will," he said. "I—I don't know what happened."

"If it happens again, Hank," Cherry said, "I'm gonna kill you myself. Do you understand that?"

"I understand, Will, I sure do."

"And no more whiskey!"

As Cherry started to walk away, Hank Wood shouted, "Wait, Will. You can't mean that!"

Cherry stopped at the bar and told the bartender, "If that man gets a drink, it means your life. Understand?"

"Sure, Mr. Cherry," the barkeep said. "Sure, I understand."

"Will!" Hank Wood cried out. "I need a drink, Will. I can't live without whiskey."

"Then you'll die," Cherry said and walked out with Sangster right behind him.

"You know you should have killed him, Will," the younger man said.

"I know."

"Will you if he takes another drink?"

"Yes," Cherry said, "and the man who gives it to him."

Another man came running up, calling Cherry's name.

"What is it, Lundy?"

"A rider approaching," Lundy said.

"Alone?"

"Yeah."

"Who spotted him?"

"Carter."

"Did he see him with a long glass?"

"Yep."

"Know him?"

"Nope."

"Okay, keep an eye on him."

"What do we do with him?"

"Watch him. He'll either head for the livery, the hotel, or the saloon. Tell the men who are stationed there."

"Yes, sir."

Cherry turned to Sangster and said, "I want to know if anyone recognizes him."

"When do we move on him?"

"When I say so."

Sangster nodded.

"I'll be at the sheriff's office," Cherry said. "Nobody moves until I say so," he reminded Sangster.

"I know, Will," Sangster said, "I know."

FIFTEEN

Clint knew he was being watched.

Aside from the fact that he was sure Cherry would have men on watch, he had seen the sun reflect off the lens of a telescope.

He wondered how they had been greeting new arrivals, and how they were going to greet him. He decided that they probably didn't reveal themselves until they'd ascertained what the new arrival was going to do. Clint actually found himself interested in how they had managed to bottle up an entire town that must have had a sheriff and deputies, and at least *some* men who could fire a gun.

As he approached the main street, he saw the man on the roof watching him. He rode down the center of the street as if he were aware of nothing. There was a man standing off the one side, and he reined Duke around so he could approach him. Clint had considered not taking Duke into the captured town, but on the off chance that he was recognized, someone might wonder why he wasn't riding his big black gelding.

The man on the street obviously didn't know how to handle Clint's approach, and stood stock-still in puzzlement.

"Excuse me."

"Me?" the man asked.

"Yes, you. Could you direct me to the livery?"

"Uh, sure, just down the street and to your right."

"Thanks," Clint said. "Right quiet town you got here."

"Yeah," the man said. "Quiet."

Clint continued and found the livery. There were two men there, one was obviously the liveryman, the other was lounging off to one side, just watching.

"C–can I help you?" the liverman said.

"You can put up my horse," Clint said, dismounting.

"Uh, sure, mister. F–for how long?"

"I don't rightly know," Clint said. "I guess that depends on how well I like your town, doesn't it?"

"Uh, I reckon that's right," the man said, taking Duke's reins.

"Treat him good, huh?" Clint said.

"Whatever you say, mister."

Clint took his rifle and saddlebags and said, "Which way to the hotel?"

"Did you come down Main Street?"

"Yep."

"Then you passed it."

"Did I? I must've missed it. Thanks again."

"Sure, mister, sure."

Clint walked through town and still didn't see a soul on the street. Granted it was early, but even this early most towns had some activity. He found the hotel and went in.

There were two men in the lobby. One was behind the desk, obviously the clerk. The other was just standing off to one side, watching.

"C–can I help you, mister?" the clerk asked nervously.

"I'd like a room."

"F–for how long?"

"Does it matter?" Clint asked. "Do I get a different room if I'm staying more than one day?"

The man laughed uneasily and said, "All the rooms are the same."

"Then I'll take one."

"Yes, sir."

The man turned the register around, and Clint simply signed, "C. Adams, Texas." There were a lot of people named Adams in the world.

"Thanks," he said, taking the key.

He turned to go to the steps and found the other man standing in his way.

"Excuse me," he said.

They exchanged stares for a few moments, and then the man stepped aside. He was the same type as the man who had been watching at the livery—young and full of himself. He must have been instructed to avoid contact with the stranger, for now.

Clint went upstairs to his room and dropped his gear on the bed. He walked to the window and looked down at the empty street.

From what he had seen, Geneva was a beautiful town. The buildings were all clean, and he had seen no sign of disrepair anywhere.

There was also no outward sign that anything was amiss, except for the empty streets.

Well, he was in. Now he'd wait a little while before going out to get something to eat.

"Where is he?" Cherry asked Sangster.

They were in the sheriff's office. The sheriff, a big, rawboned man in his fifties, was seated behind his desk. Cherry looked on the man with kindness because they were contemporaries, and the sheriff apparently knew his job.

"He's in his room at the hotel."

"Where'd he go?"

"Just the livery and the hotel."

"Anybody recognize him?"

"No."

"How did he register?"

"C. Adams."

"Adams," Will Cherry said, frowning. "He talk to anybody?"

"He spoke to Cochran, asked him where the livery was."

"That's all?"

"That's all," Sangster said, then remembered, "Oh, yeah, he told Cochran this here was a right quiet town."

Cherry rubbed his jaw and said, "He don't know the half of it."

SIXTEEN

Clint left the hotel in search of something to eat. He wasn't really hungry—he'd had at least half a breakfast at the Rogers house—but it was what a man would do when he first came into a town.

He asked the clerk for the nearest cafe and the man managed to stammer out some directions, which he now followed. The cafe was small, and when he walked in it was empty.

There was a curtained doorway in the back which probably led to the kitchen, and a middle-aged woman came through it. Looking behind her he could see that the curtain had not quite closed all the way. Another watchdog, no doubt.

"Mister?" she said.

"I'd like some eggs and coffee."

"Anything else?"

"Biscuits, if you have them."

"Oh, we got 'em," she said.

Sure you've got them, Clint said. Business had probably gone down since the takeover.

Clint sat at a table against the wall, where he had a clear view of the front door and the street out the window. He was served breakfast and ate it in peace, with no one else entering the place.

He was anxious to see if the streets would get busy at all later in the day.

He paid for his breakfast and left. He decided to take a turn around town.

All of the stores were open—the hardware store, the general store, the haberdasher's, the gunsmith— but none of them had any customers. He looked inside and saw someone behind the desk of each store, but no watchdogs. Obviously, Cherry had placed one of his men in every place he thought a stranger would go upon arriving in town—the livery, the hotel, the cafe and, later, when it opened, probably the saloon.

Clint decided to go back to his room and wait until morning eased into afternoon, and then he'd check out the saloons in town.

Sooner or later Cherry had to get curious enough to come take a look at the stranger, himself.

Maybe then things would begin to happen.

The next time Sangster went into the sheriff's office, he found Cherry and the sheriff playing two-handed poker.

"Where is he now?" Cherry asked.

Standing behind him, Sangster could see that Cherry had a straight to the ace.

"He had breakfast in the cafe and then took a turn around town."

"And?"

"And he went back to his hotel."

"Talk to anybody?"

"Just the waitress at the cafe."

"Anybody recognize him?"

"Nope."

"Call," the sheriff said after Cherry bet five dollars.

"Straight to the ace," Cherry said, spreading his cards on the man's desk.

"No good," the sheriff said. "Full house, nine's over fours."

"Damn," Cherry said. To Sangster—without looking at him—he said, "All right, keep an eye on him. He's got to come out sometime for a drink. Let me know when he does."

"All right, Will."

After Sangster left, Cherry said, "Your deal, Sheriff."

"What if he's the one?" the sheriff asked, gathering up the cards.

"Which one?" Cherry asked.

"The man who's gonna take this town back from you."

"You still think Rogers ain't gonna pay, don't you, Rivkin?"

"I do," Sheriff Tom Rivkin said.

"And you think he's gonna send somebody in here to take his town back?"

"Yes."

"One man?"

"The right man."

"You're a smart man, Sheriff. You're trying to make me nervous."

"Maybe."

"I spent fifteen years in prison, Sheriff," Cherry said, accepting his cards. "Ain't nothin' in this world can make me nervous."

Rivkin studied Cherry for a few moments and then said, "You don't care whether he pays or not, do you?"

Cherry didn't answer.

"It doesn't matter to you one way or the other, does it?" Rivkin went on. He thought he was beginning to understand Will Cherry. "Hell, even if he pays you the money you'll burn this town, won't you?"

Cherry looked at the sheriff over his cards, smiled, and said, "To the ground, Sheriff, right down to the ground. I open for ten dollars."

SEVENTEEN

With the stranger in his room and Will Cherry losing at poker to the sheriff, Johnny Sangster decided it was time to go and see Sunny Davis. He'd been thinking about her ever since he'd walked in on Cherry plowing Nina. In the past he'd walked in on them naked—and seeing Nina that way was always a pleasure—but now that he'd walked in on them in action he could no longer wait for Sunny Davis to come around to his way of thinking.

He was going to have to force the issue.

Sunny Davis sat in her room in the house she and her father, the mayor, shared. Her father was gone for the day, as usual. Even though the town was

"Under siege," as he called it, he insisted on going to his office every day.

Normally, Sunny spent her days shopping or visiting some of her friends or riding. Geneva was a beautiful town, but there wasn't much for a healthy twenty-year-old girl to do.

She thought about John Sangster. When he first rode into town she thought that perhaps he'd be an interesting companion. He was handsome, and he was new. She spent some time talking to him, and after a lot of eye contact, believed that perhaps something interesting might evolve. He was very different from the young men who lived in town.

She had no idea how different.

Then the other man came to town, Will Cherry. He was an older, brutal-looking man, and he had some sort of hold over Sangster. She wondered what kind of man John Sangster would be if he broke free of Will Cherry.

Soon all of the other men rode in, and suddenly the town was in their grasp. Will Cherry had ordered the town council to gather at the town hall, and then announced that the town was his. If anyone stood up to them, they'd be killed, otherwise no one would be hurt as long as they were there. When her father had asked how long that would be, Cherry had laughed and said, "As long as it takes to take the heart right out of Sam Rogers."

Obviously, Cherry had a score to settle with Sam Rogers, and the people of Geneva—and the entire town itself—were going to be used as pawns. The mayor had advised everyone to go along with things to keep anyone from being hurt.

"Dad," she had asked him, "shouldn't we put up

some kind of resistance? We have a sheriff, and he has deputies. We have to be able to do something."

"They have more guns than we can put together, honey," her father had said. "We're going to have to wait for Sam Rogers to take care of this himself."

Sunny looked at herself in her mirror now and wondered when Sam Rogers was going to do that.

She heard the insistent knocking on the front door downstairs and went to answer it.

When Sunny Davis opened the door Johnny Sangster was again struck by how lovely she was.

"What do you want?" she demanded.

"Is that any way to answer the door?" he asked. "I came to visit."

"I'm not accepting any visit from you, Sangster."

Sangster leaned against the wall and said, "When I first came to town you were calling me Johnny."

"That was before."

"Before what?"

"Before you and your friends took over our town and started threatening people."

"Have I threatened anyone?"

"Your friend Will Cherry said that anyone who resisted would be killed. You don't call that a threat?"

"That's his threat, not mine."

"And you're his man."

"Why don't you let me come in and we'll talk about this in more comfortable fashion?"

"I don't want you in my house," she said, and started closing the door.

Sangster blocked the door with his foot and said, "I'm afraid you don't have much choice."

She looked down at his foot and then glared at him.

"I see you've decided to stop playing at being the gentleman."

"That wasn't really getting me anywhere, was it, Sunny?" he asked. He put his hand against the door and shoved it fully open.

"I've decided to stop playing, at all."

Clint took another look out his window. There was still no activity on the streets. Apparently Cherry was making no attempt to have the town appear to be operating normally. He must have felt that everyone would be easier to control indoors.

Clint wondered what kind of sheriff Geneva had, and if he'd be able to rely on him when the time came to make a move.

He should have asked Sam Rogers about that, but since he hadn't, he decided to go over and talk to whoever was wearing the badge in Geneva.

EIGHTEEN

"Upstairs."

Sunny wondered what her chances were of breaking for the door and getting away from Sangster.

"Don't try to run, Sunny," Sangster said. "Let's just go upstairs and . . . talk."

"If you want to talk we can do it down here."

He moved up close to her and took her face in his hands, squeezing her cheeks.

"Upstairs."

For the first time, she found herself really afraid of Johnny Sangster.

Clint found the sheriff's office and looked in the window before entering. From the description Sam

Rogers had given him, it looked like the man playing cards with the sheriff was Will Cherry himself.

Let's get this underway, he thought, and opened the door.

"You don't want to do this, Johnny," Sunny Davis complained.

"Get undressed."

"Get away from Will Cherry," she said. "You're not the same kind of man he is."

Sangster closed the distance between them and slapped her across the face. Sunny cried out in pain and shock and put her hand to her cheek.

"Get undressed, or I'll tear the clothes off you," Sangster said.

Sunny saw the feverish look in his eyes and the way his breathing had accelerated. The bulge was quite evident against the front of his pants, and he was licking his lips in anticipation.

Sunny Davis was not a virgin, but neither was she very experienced.

The prospect of rape frightened her half to death.

However, the prospect of death frightened her even more.

She began to undress.

The sheriff looked up as Clint entered the office, but Will Cherry kept looking as his cards.

"Must be a good hand," Clint said.

"It'll do," Cherry said, without looking around.

"Something I can do for you?" the sheriff asked.

"Well, I'm a stranger, I just got to town and I thought I'd check in with the local law. That's you, right? Or are you a deputy?"

"I'm Sheriff Rivkin."

"This must be one of your deputies."

Clint was hoping Cherry would turn around so he could see his face, but no such luck. Not only didn't Cherry turn, but he didn't speak again, either.

"What's your name?" the sheriff asked.

"Adams."

"Well, Mr. Adams, Geneva's kind of a quiet town, and we like to keep it that way. That's the only rule a stranger has to know."

"I see," Clint said. "Well, I think I can successfully remember that."

"Good."

"I didn't mean to interrupt your game."

"That's all right."

"Excuse me," Clint said. He opened the door and left, and still Cherry hadn't turned his head.

"So?" Will Cherry said.

"So what?"

"Did you recognize him?" Cherry asked.

"No," Rivkin said.

"I'll take two cards."

Sunny was naked, and Johnny Sangster's eyes were threatening to bug out of his head.

Her skin was flawless. Her breasts were large, round, and firm, with pink nipples. Her belly was flat, and he felt as if her navel was looking straight at him. The hair between her legs was even a paler gold than the hair on her head. Her eyes, big and blue, betrayed the fear she was feeling, and that excited him even more. Her lips, slightly apart, were full and quivering slightly.

He knew just where he wanted those lips.

"I tried to be nice," he said, unbuckling his gun belt and dropping it to the floor, "but you wouldn't let me, would you?" He unbuckled his belt and began to lower his pants. "Now we have to do it the hard way, but you know what? I don't mind."

He kicked his pants away and then dropped his underwear and did the same. His erection stood out long and hard, and her eyes widened.

"Come over here."

"John—"

"Don't make me come over there, Sunny."

She lowered her head and walked toward him, stopping right in front of him. He unbuttoned his shirt and tossed it aside. Breathing heavily he put his hands on her breasts, rubbing the palms over the nipples until they began to harden.

"Yeah," he said, "yeah, you're gonna like this, I can tell."

He cupped her firm breasts in his hands, enjoying the way her smooth, warm flesh felt. He used his thumbs to flick her nipples, and she closed her eyes and bit her bottom lip. In spite of the situation, the sensation was not unpleasant, but she tried not to react to it.

He slid his hands up the slopes of her breasts, across her shoulder blades, and then let them rest on her shoulders. He exerted pressure then until she could no longer stand and fell to her knees.

"Lick it," he said.

"Please," she said, looking away from his huge erection, "I've never—"

"Believe me," he said, "you're gonna like it. I promise . . ."

NINETEEN

After Clint left the sheriff's office, he decided to go see the mayor. He doubted that he would find the mayor alone, but it was worth the chance.

He had passed the town council building when he'd made his circuit of the town, so he knew where it was. He entered, did not find the mayor's office on the first floor, and ascended to the second, where he found a door marked MAYOR DAVIS.

He entered and found himself in an outer office. There was a desk there, and seated in it was a young man in the same mold as the men he had seen at the livery and hotel.

"Can I help you?" the man asked.

"I'd like to see the mayor."

"He's busy."

"If you'll just tell him I'm here—"

"Actually, he's not here."

"Where would he be?"

"He forgot some papers at home and went to get them."

"Where does he live?"

The man hesitated. His orders obviously didn't include the answer to that question.

Finally he said, "He has a house at the northern end of town."

"Thank you." He went to the door, then turned and said, "No offense but the mayor sure has poor taste in secretaries."

"Relax," Sangster told Sunny Davis, "relax and you won't choke. That's it, relax and let it slide in and out. Yeah, that's it, you lovely animal."

Sunny bobbed her head back and forth, allowing Sangster's swollen organ to slide between her lips, in and out.

"Suck, baby, suck!" he told her.

She began to suck him and felt his hands close over her head, showing her the proper rhythm to keep.

"Keep those teeth to yourself, Sunny," he warned her. "You bite me and you'll be sorry."

The thought had occured to her, but her fear of him was too great, so she continued to suck on him, wondering what she would do if he shot his load into her mouth. My God, she could suffocate.

She felt his penis swelling in her mouth and panicked, but he pulled her head away, freeing himself from her mouth.

"All right, on the bed, Sunny. Let's get to it."

"Please, John—"

He slapped her then and said, "You call me Mr. Sangster! Now get on that bed!" He shoved her, and she fell back across the bed, whimpering.

He got on the bed with her and pressed his face to her breasts. He sucked her nipples while he inserted two fingers inside her vagina. Sunny began to squirm, digging her buttocks into the bedsheets.

"You're starting to like it, aren't you?"

"No!" she shouted.

It was a lie, and it wasn't. Although she wasn't exactly liking it, her body was reacting to the things he was doing, and there was no way she could control that.

His mouth was moving over her now, lower and lower until his face was pressed into her pubic hair. She felt his tongue penetrate her, and immediately climaxed. No man had ever done that to her before! Even as she experienced the biggest orgasm of her life, she felt ashamed. Sangster was not the man she'd wanted this to happen with.

He continued licking her and she squirmed and moaned as he built her toward another climax. When he centered his attention on her clit, licking and sucking, she lifted her buttocks off the bed and shuddered as she came again—this one even more intense than the last.

Sangster couldn't believe how good she tasted. He couldn't get enough of her. He kept licking and sucking and lapping at her like a starving dog, and then he knelt between her legs, grabbed her ankles and spread her wide open. Her womanhood was pink and moist, and his eyes shone as he said with delight, "Now!"

"Sunny!" Mayor Davis called as he entered the house. "Are you here, Sunny?"

Sunny opened her mouth to answer, but Sangster quickly covered her mouth with his hand.

"Not a sound," he said. "You don't want your father to get hurt, do you?"

She shook her head, her eyes wide with fright.

"Good, then just lie still and enjoy it."

He removed his hand from her mouth, lifted his hips and rammed his penis into her. She climaxed immediately, biting her lip to suppress a scream.

"Ooh, God," he whispered in her ear, "it's like sticking it in a vat of hot butter, girl!"

"Sunny!" her father called. He was in the hallway outside the door now, and they could both hear him muttering. "That girl is out spending my money again. Ah, hell, where did I leave those papers?"

Sangster slid his hands beneath Sunny and cupped her smooth, tight buttocks, pulling her tightly to him so he penetrated her even deeper. As if they had a life of their own, her legs lifted up and wrapped themselves around his hips. Her arms went around him and she began to rake his back with her nails. It was getting harder and harder for her to keep silent, but she felt as if her father's life might depend on it.

"Shh," he said into her ear, "just enjoy it."

Clint found the house, and since it was the biggest one he saw, he assumed it was the mayor's. He mounted the front steps and knocked.

* * *

Upstairs in his bedroom Mayor Davis heard the knocking and left his room to answer it. As he passed his daughter's room, though, he heard sounds from inside. Someone was moaning, and bedsprings were screaming.

"What the—" he said. She's never brought a man here before, he thought. How dare she, especially with what's been going on.

The mayor stepped to his daughter's bedroom door and slammed the door open.

"What the hell is going on?" he demanded.

The tableau before him made his blood run cold. A man he recognized as Johnny Sangster—Will Cherry's right-hand man—was atop his daughter on her bed, and both were naked.

Sunny turned her face toward her father and from the expression there he knew that whatever was happening, his daughter was not willing.

"Daddy!" she screamed.

"Get off her, you animal!" the mayor shouted.

Now Mayor Davis was almost sixty, and was medium-sized, while Sangster was in his mid-twenties and strong. Throughout his life, Davis had not been a physical man, but he rushed forward now, grabbed Sangster around the waist and lifted him off his daughter, depositing him on the floor with a thud.

"Daddy—" Sunny cried, and Davis sat on the bed and put his arms protectively around her.

Sangster stood up in a rage.

"You son of a bitch!" he shouted. He began to look around for his gun and when he spotted it, he stooped to pick it up.

"I wouldn't," a voice called out from the door.

The naked Sangster looked toward the door and saw someone standing there. It was the stranger who had ridden into town that morning.

"Get out of here!" Sangster shouted.

"I think you should get dressed," the man said. "You look ridiculous."

"This is none of your business," Sangster said. He reached for his gun and closed his hand around the butt. Before he could draw it . . . a foot came down on his hand, pinning it.

"Mr. Mayor?"

"Yes," Davis said.

"Would you toss this man's clothing out the window, please?"

Davis smiled and said, "It would be my pleasure."

"No," Sangster shouted as Davis scooped up his clothes and walked to the window. The mayor opened the window and dropped Sangster's clothes outside.

"And now his gun."

Davis pulled Sangster's gun from beneath his hand and tossed it out the window.

Clint stepped back, removing his foot from Sangster's hand.

Sangster stood up, rubbing his hand.

"Do you know who I am?"

"A bully, and a rapist, from what I can see. Now you'd better get going before somebody steals your clothes."

"You ain't heard the last of this, friend," Sangster said menacingly.

"Somehow you being naked takes something away from your threats," Clint said. "Come back when you're dressed."

Sangster stood there and shook with rage, then turned and stalked out of the room.

"Mister, I don't know who you are," Davis said, covering his daughter with a sheet, "but we owe you our lives."

"Mr. Mayor," Clint said, "while we're alone, I think we should talk."

TWENTY

Sangster charged into the sheriff's office and slammed the door behind him. He was disheveled, having dressed hastily outside the mayor's house, before someone could see him.

"I'm gonna kill him!"

Rivkin looked up and said, "You look agitated."

"Kill who?" Will Cherry asked.

"That stranger!"

Cherry put his cards down and turned in his chair to look at Sangster.

"You had contact with him?"

Much of Sangster's initial anger melted beneath Will Cherry's hard gaze.

"My orders were no contact."

"I know . . . I know . . ." Sangster said. "I didn't cause the contact, he did."

"How?"

"I was . . . visiting Sunny Davis—"

"Where?"

"At her house."

"Did she invite you?"

"Yeah . . . sure . . ."

"Johnny."

"Well, not exactly."

"How did the stranger get involved?"

Sangster groped for an answer that wouldn't incriminate him.

Cherry stood up and approached him.

"Where did you leave him?"

"At the mayor's house."

"Who's there?"

"Sunny, the stranger . . . and the mayor."

"And the mayor is not covered?"

"Well . . ."

Cherry whirled on the sheriff and said, "Don't leave your office!" He turned back to Sangster and said, "Come on!"

Clint waited in the hall while Sunny Davis quickly got dressed, and then the three of them went downstairs.

Clint walked to the window and said, "I don't know how much time we have."

"Who are you?" Mayor Davis asked.

"My name is Clint Adams," Clint said. "I'm working for Sam Rogers."

"You're here to help?" Sunny Davis asked.

"Yes, ma'am," he said. "Excuse me, but do you need a doctor?"

"No, I'm all right," she said.

"To answer your question, yes, I'm here to help."

"But . . . what can one man do?" she asked.

"My dear," the mayor said, "didn't you hear his name?"

"Yes, Clint Adams. What—"

"Clint Adams . . . the Gunsmith," the mayor said. He looked at Clint and said, "Isn't that correct?"

"I've been called that, yes."

"Called that?" the mayor said. "*Are* you the Gunsmith?"

"I don't think I want to discuss that now, Mr. Mayor," Clint said. "I don't think we have time to discuss who you think I am, and who I think I am. Do you have any men who can shoot, who can be ready when I need them?"

"Do I have men?" the mayor asked. "What about Sam Rogers? Does he have men?"

"I have men waiting on the outside," Clint said. "What I need to know is, do I have men on the inside. For instance, is the sheriff reliable?"

"Rivkin's always been reliable . . . in the past," the mayor said.

Clint was about to ask what "in the past" meant, when the front door slammed open.

Will Cherry stood just inside the door with Johnny Sangster at his side.

Sunny Davis caught her breath and her father put his arm around her.

Clint regarded them both easily and then said to Sangster, "I see you decided to get dressed."

"What does that mean?" Will Cherry asked, as if he didn't like something going on that he didn't know about.

"Ask your boy," Clint said. "Seems he likes running around without his clothes on."

Cherry examined the faces of everyone in the room, and then turned his gaze on Sangster.

"I don't know what he's talking about."

"What happened here?" Cherry asked.

"I didn't—" Sangster said, but Cherry cut him off.

"I'm asking them."

"You're right-hand man here decided it was time to rape my daughter."

Clint could see the look in Will Cherry's eyes. Cherry was an old-timer, and had an old-timer's regard for women. As ruthless as he might have been, he wouldn't stand for rape.

"Is that true?" Cherry asked Sunny.

"Hey, Will—" Sangster started.

"I'm asking her!" Cherry snapped.

Sunny looked at Sangster, Cherry, and her father, but it wasn't until she looked at Clint and he nodded that she gave Cherry his answer.

"Yes."

Faster than any of them could follow, Cherry lashed out and hit Sangster a backhanded blow across the face. Sangster staggered back, a look of shock on his face, but Cherry wasn't done. He turned and hit Sangster in the stomach with his fist, doubling the younger man over. He grabbed a handful of Sangster's hair then and yanked the man's head up.

"Do you remember what you said I should do to Hank Wood, Johnny?" he asked.

"Wha—"

"Hank killed a woman," Cherry said, "but to me, rape is even worse than that."

Clint decided that Cherry had a warped sense of propriety.

"From now on you stay away from the mayor's daughter, and every other woman in town. Do you understand?"

"I . . . understand . . ." Sangster said, still breathless from the blow to the stomach.

"Now get out!" Cherry said, pushing the man toward the front door, where he staggered outside.

Will Cherry walked up to Sunny Davis then, where she sat on the couch.

"Miss Davis, I'm sorry for what happened."

"Why can't you just let this town alone?" she asked.

Cherry smiled and said, "I wish I could, I really do, but I need to hold it for just a little while longer."

Cherry nodded to the mayor and then turned to Clint.

"Could I buy you a drink?"

"Sure," Clint said, "why not? Is the saloon open?"

"Don't worry," Cherry said. "We'll open it."

TWENTY-ONE

Clint and Will Cherry left the mayor's house together, heading for the saloon.

"I guess you're a bit curious about what's going on in this town," Cherry said.

"Some," Clint said. "What did the mayor's daughter mean when she said you should let the town go?"

"We can talk about that when we get to the saloon," Cherry said. "I think I might have a proposition for you."

"You don't even know me."

"You obviously got the best of Sangster," Cherry said, "and he was my top man."

"If he's your top man, you're in trouble."

"Maybe I'm starting to realize that," Cherry said.

They reached the saloon and were admitted after Cherry banged on the door.

"Looks like business is slow," Clint said to the bartender.

"It's as slow or fast as Mr. Cherry says," the man said sullenly.

"Bring us a couple of beers, Dave."

"My name's not Dave," the bartender said, but he shuffled off to get the beer.

When Clint and Cherry each had a beer, Cherry introduced himself.

"My name's Will Cherry."

"Seems to me I've heard that name before," Clint said, and then added, "but not for some years."

"Fifteen," Cherry said. "What's your name?"

"Adams."

"That's what it says on the hotel register," Cherry said, "C. Adams. What does the C. stand for—" But before Clint could answer, a look of comprehension came over Cherry's face.

"Wait a minute," he said, "*Clint* Adams?"

"That's right."

"The Gunsmith?"

"I prefer to be called by my name."

"Even inside we've heard about you. You were a lawman when I went inside, weren't you?"

"Fifteen years ago?" Clint said. "I think I was out of it by then."

"Why?"

"I got tired of it. There wasn't any money to be had."

"And what are you doing now?"

"Drifting," Clint said, "and there's no money in that, either."

"What are you doing in Geneva?" Cherry asked.

"Passing through."

"On the way to where?"

"Like I said," Clint said, "I'm drifting."

Cherry rubbed his jaw and studied Clint. Clint knew what he was thinking. He'd been inside a long time and didn't know in any detail what Clint had been doing for the past fifteen years.

"What's going on here?" Clint asked.

"I don't think I'm gonna answer that yet, Clint. Let's just say I've got this town bottled up tight."

"I got in," Clint said.

"Without my say-so, you can't get out," Cherry said.

"I don't like being told what I can and can't do, Cherry."

"That's too bad," Cherry said, standing up, "because this town is mine, Adams. I'm not even going to take your gun, because you couldn't get out of town if you tried."

"I see."

"My advice is not to try," Cherry said. "You might find it profitable to stay here willingly."

"And when will I know whether or not I have that option?" Clint asked.

"In a while," Cherry said. "I have some people to talk to, first."

"Like Sangster?"

"I had Sangster figured wrong," Cherry said. "I thought he was like me, but I'd never rape a woman."

"You'd kill one, though."

"If I had to," Cherry said, "but I wouldn't violate her first. No man should do that to a woman who isn't willing."

"Well, we agree on that, anyway."

"We may even agree on a lot more," Cherry said. "We'll have to wait and see."

Cherry headed for the front door and called out to the bartender, "You can open, Dave, and bring my friend another beer."

The bartender brought Clint a beer and was muttering, "Open, close, what's the difference. Nobody comes in—nobody who pays, anyway."

"Who comes in?"

"Just Cherry's men," the bartender said, "and they don't pay."

"What about the townspeople?"

"They're not allowed on the streets. We're the only ones allowed to come out, and that's just to open up."

"Who do you mean?"

"All of us—the businessmen. We have to be open in case Cherry's men want something."

"Tell me something."

The bartender looked around, saw that no one else was present or coming in, and said, "Sure, why not?"

"I heard something about a man killing a woman."

"Yeah, one of Cherry's men got too drunk to use a whore the proper way, so he beat her to death."

"What did Cherry do to him?"

"The fella's a drunk, so Cherry cut off his liquor."

"Where is the man now?"

"Probably crawled into a hole somewhere and pulled it in after him."

"Has anyone else been hurt since they've been here?"

"A couple of bruises maybe, a broken arm or two, but nothing serious. That was all during the first day they were here. Everybody seemed to get the message after that."

"Yeah, I guess they would."

"You gonna join him?" the bartender asked.

"I haven't been asked."

"I heard him say who you were, Mr. Adams," the bartender said. "You could help this town."

"Not all alone I couldn't."

"Well . . . if you decide you want to, and you need any help, you ask for me, hear?"

"I'll keep that in mind."

The bartender nodded and started to go back to the bar.

"Hey," Clint said.

"What?"

"If your name's not Dave, what is it?"

The bartender smiled and said, "Ethan."

"Ethan?" Clint said. "I can almost see why he prefers to call you Dave."

"You know what," Ethan said, "so can I."

Out on the street Cherry grabbed the first one of his men he could find, a man named Forrest.

"Find me Malone and Carter and tell them I want to see them at the hotel—now!"

"Yes, sir."

Will Cherry turned and looked at the saloon. Having the Gunsmith ride into town was an interesting turn of events. Now it remained to be seen whether it was going to be a problem or an advantage.

TWENTY-TWO

When Cherry entered his room Nina got up off the bed where she'd been sitting to greet him. He went past her without seeing her.

"Will."

He turned and focused on her, as if seeing her for the first time.

"What?"

"What's wrong?"

"Nothing," he said. "Go take a walk, I have some men coming over."

"I'll stay, and help."

"What?"

"I said I'd like to help."

"I don't need your help, Nina," he said.

"Oh, no?" she said. "You only need me when you want to go to bed, is that it?"

"That's it," he said. "That's what I brought you along for. Didn't you know that?"

"Yes, I knew it, but I thought—"

"Thought what?"

"Thought that maybe . . ."

"Nina, you aren't really equipped to think," Cherry said. "You're real well equipped for bed, though, and I'll tell you when I need you for that."

"You should try bringing some feelings to bed with you sometime!" she said.

"Get out, now. I have some business."

"Sure," she said, "sure, take care of your business."

Since she was already dressed in a shirt and jeans, she pulled on her boots, grabbed her hat, and stormed from the room, slamming the door behind her.

Moments later there was a knock at the door. When it opened, both Frank Carter and Dan Malone entered.

"What's wrong with Nina?" Carter asked.

"You'd better keep that little filly a lot happier, Will," Malone said.

Carter and Malone were the same age and Cherry, early fifties. Carter was tall and skinny, which made his large, knobby-knuckled hands seem even larger. Malone had put weight on over the years and now toted around thirty pounds too much for his five-feet-nine, all of it in his gut.

"What's wrong, Will?" Carter asked.

"Stranger came to town today."

"We heard."

"He's not a stranger anymore."

Malone and Carter exchanged glances and then Malone said, "Who is he?"

"Clint Adams."

"Adams?" Malone said.

"The Gunsmith?" Carter said.

"He prefers to be called by his name.'

"What's he doing here?" Malone asked.

"Passing through . . . he says."

"You got cause to believe different?" Malone asked.

"That's what I wanted to ask you two."

"Why us?"

"Because I've been inside for fifteen years," Cherry said. "Tell me what the Gunsmith has been doing for all that time."

"How would we know?" Malone asked.

"You can read can't you?" Cherry asked them. "You've seen newspapers. Is he the kind of man who would join us if I offered it to him?"

The two men exchanged a glance again.

"Well, he hasn't worn a badge in all that time that I heard," Malone said.

"And he hasn't robbed any banks."

"He's made the newspapers, hasn't he?" Cherry asked.

"He has," Malone said, "but who believes what you read in the newspaper?"

"You've got a point there," Cherry said. "Have either of you ever met him personally?"

Malone shook his head and Carter said, "No, but you do have someone in town who has."

"Who?"

"Henry Wood."

"Hank? He's met the Gunsmith?"

"A few years back, I think," Malone said, "but he still might be able to tell you more about the kind of man he is that we can."

"Find him," Cherry said.

"Nobody's seen him since you . . . you took him off the bottle."

"Find him."

"He may not talk without a drink, Will," Carter said warningly.

"If he needs one I'll be the one to give it to him," Cherry said, "but find him and bring him to me."

"We'll find him," Malone said, "but I don't know how much good he'll be."

"As good as dead, maybe," Carter said, but Cherry didn't hear him.

Which was just as well.

At that moment Hank Wood was lying in a stall in the livery stable, facedown in a pile of horseshit, oblivious to that fact. He was not drunk, he was unconscious. Since Cherry had forbidden him to have any liquor, he had also not had any food. Since Cherry had forbidden him from any of the town's saloons, he had no place to sleep.

He was as totally unaware of his surroundings, as if he were dead.

Clint Adams was still in the saloon, working on another beer. Two of Cherry's men had come in, gotten a bottle of whiskey, and then taken a table. He wondered if Cherry had sent them over to keep an eye on him. The way to find out would be to leave and see if they followed, but he didn't have anyplace to go.

The next move was Cherry's, and he thought he might as well wait right where he was for him to make it.

TWENTY-THREE

Nina Engel went down to the hotel dining room after leaving Will Cherry's room. She was looking around for a table when she saw Johnny Sangster sitting alone at a table, looking something less than happy.

"Mind a little company?" she asked, approaching his table.

He looked up at her and she could see the bruise on his face.

"What happened to you?" she asked, sitting down.

"Your friend has a quick temper," Sangster said.

"Will hit you?"

"Right."

"Why?"

"I told you," Sangster said, "he's got a quick temper. He doesn't know who his friends are."

"You're right about that," she said.

Her tone made him perk up with interest.

"What are you doing down here?"

"He kicked me out of the room."

"Why?"

"He said he was meeting with some men."

"Probably Malone and Carter," Sangster said. "He seems to feel that because they're his age they're better than the rest of us."

"I thought you were his number-one man?"

"I thought so, too," Sangster said. "I thought you were his number-one girl."

"He only needs me when he's in the mood for sex," she said. "Other than that, I don't exist."

It was obvious to him that she was as unhappy with Will Cherry as he was at that moment.

Johnny Sangster looked across the table at her and asked, "What do you see in him, anyway? He's old enough to be your father."

"Well, in the beginning he was interesting," she said. "You know, he just got out of jail after fifteen years and—my God, he was able to go on forever . . . if you know what I mean . . ."

"I know what you mean," he said, "but Christ, you could find a lot of younger men who can do that."

"Well, I haven't found a lot up to now," she said, giving him a speculative look.

He noticed the interested look she was giving him now. He also noticed she had beautiful blue eyes, and a full, generous mouth. He remembered the times he'd seen her nude, and the expression on her face the last time he'd seen her, with Will Cherry's penis buried in her to the hilt.

Also, the idea of bedding down Will Cherry's girl suddenly appealed to him.

"Maybe you haven't been looking in the right places, Nina."

TWENTY-FOUR

When the water hit Wood in the face he sputtered to some semblance of life.

"Well, at least we know he's not dead," Will Cherry said. "Throw him in the horse trough."

"He might drown," Malone said.

"Do it."

Wood, just barely aware that something was going on, moved his arms weakly as Malone and Carter lifted him, carried him to the trough, and dropped him in.

"Did you get the whiskey?" Cherry asked.

"Right here," Carter said, producing a bottle of whiskey.

Wood was moving about in the trough, splashing,

trying to get his head above the water and failing.

"Will . . ." Malone said.

"Yeah?"

"He's drowning."

"Get him out, then."

Malone and Carter hauled Wood out of the water and dumped him unceremoniously on the ground, where he lay in a puddle of his own making.

"Are you awake, Wood?" Cherry shouted.

Wood spluttered a few times, and then managed to croak out the word, "Yes."

"Do you want a drink?"

The man's eyes popped open, and he stared at Will Cherry in horror.

"A drink?"

"Yes."

"But you said—"

"Never mind what I said," Cherry said, holding the bottle where Wood could see it. "Do you want one?"

"Yes," Wood said, "Oh, yes." He made a pitiful picture, sitting on the ground in a puddle of water, reaching for the whiskey bottle.

"I need some information."

"Information?" he asked, his hand wavering. "What information?"

"About Clint Adams."

Wood frowned and said, "Clint Adams? What—I don't—"

"The man they call the Gunsmith."

Wood was trying hard to think, but it wasn't easy.

"Please, Will," he said, "I can't think. Just one little drink . . ."

"All right," Cherry said. The bottle he was holding had already been started and was only about half full. He pulled out the cork and handed Wood the bottle.

Hank Wood grabbed onto the bottle with both hands and held it so tight that Cherry thought it might shatter. He lifted it to his lips, and as the amber liquid began to pour into his mouth, Cherry grabbed the bottle and pulled it away from him. Wood gasped and reached for the bottle, then tried to catch what was left of the liquor that was rolling down his chin.

"That's all!" Cherry said. "Answer my question."

"Question? What question?"

"I want to know what you know about Clint Adams, the Gunsmith . . ."

The questioning went on in that vein for some time, Cherry feeding Wood a mouthful of liquor when the other man's memory began to cloud, showing patience when Malone and Carter would have lost theirs.

The information gleaned, however, did not do much to help Cherry make up his mind about Clint Adams. As far as Hank Wood knew, the Gunsmith had earned his reputation as the fastest gun since Wild Bill Hickok and, some people said, may have even been Hickok's equal—or better!

That was what Wood knew about Clint Adams's ability with a gun. What Will Cherry wanted to know, however, was what kind of man the Gunsmith was.

"If he rode into this situation, what would he do?" he asked Wood.

Wood shrugged and said, "Mind his business, I guess."

"Does he hire out?"

"Near as I can recall, you couldn't hire his gun."

"So if I wanted to sign him on, you don't think he would?"

Wood frowned and said, "My head hurts—"

"The quicker you answer the quicker you can curl up somewhere with this bottle!"

"As long as you ain't hiring him to kill somebody," Wood said.

"We don't want to kill anyone," Cherry said, handing Wood the bottle. "Go find a corner, Wood. Don't let me see you when you're drunk."

Wood grabbed the bottle, thanked Cherry profusely, and crawled off into the livery.

"Probably gonna find the same spot in the horseshit," Malone said, and Carter laughed.

"Don't laugh," Cherry said to them. "That could be any one of us."

Malone and Carter both sobered.

"Did talking to him help?"

"Not a whole hell of a lot," Cherry said. "I still don't know if I want to make Adams an offer to throw in with us."

"And if you don't, then what do we do? Try and hold him?" Carter asked.

"Hold the Gunsmith?" Malone said.

"Oh, we could hold him," Cherry said. "After all, he's only one man."

"One man or not, he could be trouble if he's against us," Malone said.

"It may not be a question of for or against," Cherry said. "We could let him ride on, or we could let him sit it out here with the others."

"How would he react—"

"Never mind," Cherry said, waving them away. "I'm just going to have to make up my mind myself.

You fellas get back to your posts."

"You'll let us know what happens?"

Cherry looked at them, ready to tell them that what happens was up to him and they needn't worry, but he looked at the two men—his links to his past—and said instead, "Yeah, I'll let you know."

As they walked away, he realized that if he were the kind of man who needed someone to talk to, he would talk to them, because the others were so young.

Unfortunately, he wasn't that type of man.

He was undecided about whether to go back to his hotel, or go right over to the saloon and talk to Clint Adams again. Hell, they were both in the same direction. He'd decide on the way.

Clint finally got tired of nursing beers by himself and walked to the bar.

"You got any cards, Ethan?"

"Sure," Ethan said, handing over a deck. "You gonna play with them?" He nodded toward Cherry's men.

"Why not?" Clint said. "Their money's as green as anybody else's. Give me a fresh beer, too, will you?"

Clint took the beer and the cards and walked to the table where the two men were seated.

"You fellas interested in a little poker?"

The two men exchanged glances, and then shrugged.

TWENTY-FIVE

Sangster couldn't help comparing the taste of Nina's vagina with Sunny Davis's. He had to admit that it wasn't as sweet, but Nina had Sunny beat as far as the scent. There was something about Nina's odor that appealed to him.

In fact, there was something about this whole thing that appealed to him.

They had gone right from the dining room to the hotel room and undressed. Nina had grabbed Sangster's penis right away and pulled him toward the bed. When they tumbled to the sheets together she had reversed herself and taken him in her mouth. She worked on him feverishly, and Sangster knew that he was going to have to use all of his willpower to last, because she'd be comparing him to Cherry.

Sometime later he finally lost control and flooded her mouth, and she didn't seem disappointed.

She had lain back then, spreading her legs, and he went to work on her with his mouth. When he reached her womanhood he started making comparisons of his own, and she wasn't doing too badly, either.

Still, he knew that a lot of the excitement he was feeling was from the fact that she was Will Cherry's girl.

When he entered her, slamming into her so hard that she cried out and clutched him to her, he began to take her in long, violent strokes, as if every one of them would cause Will Cherry some pain.

Will Cherry finally made up his mind where he wanted to go, only because he came to the hotel first. He still had some thinking to do before he approached Clint Adams, and he decided to do it in his room.

Maybe he'd do it after relaxing with Nina, if she was still there.

"Not bad," Nina said.

"What do you mean, not bad?" Sangster asked.

She laughed, kissed his right nipple, and said, "I'm teasing you, Johnny. It was marvelous."

"You say that like we're finished."

She looked surprised and said, "You mean we're not?"

"Not by a long sight," he said.

He got up onto his knees on the bed, grabbed her and turned her over. She knew immediately what he wanted. She got on all fours and presented him with a wonderful view of her behind.

Cherry walked through the lobby to the hotel dining room, which was empty. Even if Nina had been there, he wouldn't have known what to say to her. She was right, he didn't know how to treat people. He'd lost that somewhere in Huntsville Prison at about the three- or four-year mark of his fifteen-year stretch.

Maybe she was waiting in the room, and he wouldn't have to say anything to her at all. The girl sure loved sex, and even without emotion, he knew he was able to satisfy her.

He went upstairs.

"Come on, come on," Nina cried out as Sangster licked her slippery clitoris. "Put it in, put it in . . ."

He got high up on his knees, grabbed ahold of her hips, slid his penis between her thighs and up into her tunnel.

"Oh, Jesus, yes!" Nina said, moaning. "Yes, yes, that's it, Johnny, that's it . . ."

"Oh, yeah!" he said, agreeing with her.

This was it . . .

And then the door opened.

Both of them froze on the bed and looked at Will Cherry, standing in the doorway.

"Will," Sangster said, withdrawing from Nina, "this isn't what you think."

"That is one of the dumbest things you've ever said, Johnny," Will Cherry said, "and it will be your last."

"Will, don't!"

Sangster moved for his gun, which was hanging on the bedpost, but he wasn't nearly fast enough. Cherry drew and fired twice. The first slug killed Sangster and dumped him on top of Nina, and she felt the second slug go into his body.

She screamed and scrambled from beneath Sangster's bulk, falling to the floor. She stood up then and faced Cherry, who still had his gun out.

"Now, Will," she said, "what the hell did you do that for? You don't even care!"

"You're right," he said, "I don't."

He raised his gun to fire, and she backed away until she came to the window. He fired once, putting a bullet between her breasts. The force of the impact knocked her through the window, and she fell to the street in a shower of broken glass.

At the sound of the shots, both of Cherry's men sprang to their feet and ran for the door. The bartender and Clint exchanged glances, and then Clint got up and rushed out after them.

He saw the crowd gathering down the street in front of the hotel and slowed to a walk. When he got there he saw the naked woman lying on the street like a broken doll. He barely had time to take a look when another body came falling from a window, landing not far from the woman.

Everyone on the street looked up at the shattered window and saw Will Cherry peering down at them.

Maybe, Clint thought, looking at the two bodies, things are starting to fall apart for Will Cherry.

TWENTY-SIX

While the onlookers were waiting for Will Cherry to come downstairs, the mayor and the sheriff each showed up separately. On the other side of the crowd Clint spotted two men who were Cherry's age. He assumed that these men were Frank Carter and Dan Malone.

Some of the people in the crowd were townspeople, but for the most part the townspeople had remained inside, and the onlookers were Will Cherry's men. There must have been twenty of them there, and they were seeing two of their own number dead on the ground. How would that sit with them? That two of their own were killed by their own boss?

As he scanned Cherry's men, something occured to him. He didn't see anyone who might be the Breed.

In fact, he hadn't seen anyone like that since he'd arrived.

"What happened?" Rivkin asked, looking at Clint.

"Looks like Cherry and some of his people had a falling out," Clint said, "and judging from the conditions of the bodies, it's not hard to figure why."

Rivkin and Davis exchanged glances.

"Was that Cherry's woman?" Clint asked.

"Yes," Rivkin said.

"And that's his number-one man, Sangster," Clint said, recognizing Sangster. "I guess Cherry's got a job opening."

"Are you interested in filling it?" Rivkin asked.

"I'm interested in some quick questions before Cherry gets here."

"Go ahead," Rivkin said with hesitation.

"Can you get away at night?"

"Sure. Nobody sleeps with me."

"Mayor, can we meet at your house?"

"When?"

"Tonight."

"What about—" Davis began, but before he could finish Cherry appeared.

"Tonight, late," Clint said.

Cherry approached Sheriff Rivkin and said, "Get these people off the street."

"Most of them are yours," Rivkin pointed out.

"I'll take care of my people," Cherry said tightly, "you and the mayor take care of yours."

"Sure, Mr. Cherry," Rivkin said. "Sure."

"And get somebody to move these bodies."

"Sure."

The sheriff approached some of the people and asked them to move on.

Will Cherry turned on his people and shouted, "This isn't a circus. Get back where you belong!"

Some of them began to move away, but others remained, staring down at Sangster's body. The girl's body didn't mean that much to them, but Sangster was one of their own.

"Malone, Carter," Cherry said, "move them along."

Abruptly, Malone and Carter obeyed, getting the other men to leave.

"Maybe they feel they deserve an explanation," Mayor Davis said to Cherry.

"They deserve whatever I choose to give them," Cherry said. "You'd better get to your office, Mayor, or to your house. I want the street cleared."

Cherry turned and found himself looking at Clint Adams.

"What do you want?"

"Buy you a drink?"

Cherry stared at him for a few moments, then said, "Sure, why not?"

After the street was cleared and the bodies were moved, Malone and Carter got together in a small saloon at the south end of town.

"What do you think?" Malone asked.

"I don't know. He's been inside for a long time," Carter replied.

"You think he's crazy?"

"It's pretty obvious what happened," Carter said. "What would you do if you walked in on another man in bed with your woman?"

"I don't know," Malone said, "it's been so long since I've had a woman of my own."

• • •

In the saloon Cherry wanted whiskey, but Clint talked him into beer.

"You can cry into it and not get drunk so fast."

"Who says I'm looking to cry?" Cherry said, but he took the beer.

"What happened?" Clint asked.

"Something I never would have expected," Cherry said. "I walked in on them and killed them both. Just like that. She said I had no feelings."

"I guess she was wrong."

"No, that's the funny part of it," Cherry said. "She was right. I killed them without any feeling."

"Then . . . why?"

"Because he took something that was mine," Cherry said. "In prison, when somebody takes what's yours, you kill them."

"So why kill her?"

"Same reason."

It didn't sound quite the same to Clint, but he let it drop. It was very possible that he'd killed the woman in some kind of bloodlust, simply because she was there.

"Your men weren't very happy, Cherry."

"The hell with them," Cherry said. "They'll do what they're getting paid to do."

"And what is that?"

Cherry looked at Clint and said, "Do you really want to know?"

Clint shrugged.

"We've got to have something to talk about while we're drinking."

And the man who didn't need anyone to talk to said, "Well, why not?"

TWENTY-SEVEN

"I've got this town in a bottle."

"That's an interesting way to put it."

"It's the only way to put it," Will Cherry said. "People can get in, but they can't get out without my say-so."

"Like me?"

"Like you."

"Would you like to tell me why?"

"Sure, I'll tell you why," Cherry said. "Fifteen years ago I had a partner. We'd been riding together for about five years at that point. We shared hard times, good times, hell, we'd even shared a woman or two along the way. I thought we were friends." Cherry paused a moment, then laughed—at himself,

Clint thought—and said, "That shows you how much I knew."

Cherry fell silent then and Clint decided not to push him, to let him continue at his own pace.

Finally, he did.

"Anyway, Sam came up with a bold plan. We were gonna rob us two banks, in two different towns, on the same day—each of us single-handedly."

"I'd say that was bold," Clint agreed.

"It would make us reputations for life. Then we were going to take the money we got and start a ranch," Cherry said. "We were going to go straight."

"Together?"

"That's right," he said, "together, me and my good *friend*."

Clint hadn't heard that part of it. He was starting to get a very different picture of Sam Rogers—one which, surprisingly enough, didn't surprise him.

"And what happened?"

"What happened," Cherry repeated, shaking his head, "was, that when I got there, they were waiting for me. They let me get inside the bank, and then the sheriff and four deputies closed me up inside. There wasn't even anybody in there that I could use as a hostage. I walked into that bank, saw that it was empty, and knew they had me cold."

"They'd been tipped off." Clint asked.

Cherry laughed and said, "Oh, they'd been tipped off good and proper, and who do you think did it?"

"Your partner?"

"Who else could have?" Cherry said. "My partner, Sam Rogers, was the only one who knew I was going there."

"Did you ever find that out for sure?"

"I didn't have to," Cherry said. "I *knew!* In here," Cherry continued, pounding his chest, "I knew Sam Rogers had turned me in."

"I see."

"No, you don't see," Cherry said, standing up. "Let me get two more beers."

Cherry went to the bar and returned with two fresh beers, then continued with his story as if he'd never stopped.

"I got out of Huntsville on June first, but I had decided long before that that when I did get out I was going to get even with Sam Rogers. Well, he's a rich, important man now. He built this town, named it after his late wife. He loves this town. I found all of this out when I got out, and that's when I knew I had a way to get my revenge."

"And that's when you decided to take the town and bottle it up."

"Take it," Cherry said, "sell it back to him . . . and then burn it to the ground."

Now Clint knew very clearly what Cherry's intentions were, and it chilled him. To avenge himself on one man he was willing to destroy an entire town.

"What about the people, Cherry?"

"What about them?"

"Why should the people who live in Geneva pay for what Rogers did to you?"

There was a moment's hesitation, and then Cherry said, "Shit, why not?"

Right then and there Clint thought there might be a way to save the town that he hadn't thought of to this point.

Like talking Will Cherry out of it.

TWENTY-EIGHT

Over a few more beers Cherry told Clint how he had bottled up Geneva.

He had men at both ends of town, with instructions to let people in, but not out.

"I don't want to keep anybody out, because they might report the trouble to some other lawman in some other town," Cherry explained. "So, once they're in, I don't let them out for the same reason."

"What if they promise not to say anything?"

"I wouldn't believe them," Cherry said, "just like I wouldn't believe you."

"I wouldn't be dumb enough to think you would," Clint said.

"Anyway, once we took the sheriff and his deputies and the mayor, we had the town leaders come to a town council meeting, and explained the situation. Nobody resists, and nobody gets hurt." He paused to wet his lips with a beer. "A few people had to be convinced, but once that was done, everybody else got the idea. Now they all stay inside, except the businessmen. They stay open because my men might need something."

"You pay for what you take?"

"What do you think?"

Clint didn't answer.

"And then there's the bank."

"What about it?" Clint asked.

"Before we leave we'll clean it out. That's how I'll pay my men."

"Will there be enough money there?"

"Sam Rogers's bank? There sure will be."

"What do you mean, Rogers's bank?"

"He owns it."

If that was true, then Rogers had lied to Clint.

"Oh, he don't own it outright," Cherry said. "He's got somebody else's name on it, but he owns it, all right."

Clint finished his beer and watched Cherry finish his. They'd had about five each at this point, and neither one of them was drunk. Sometimes a man comes out of prison with less capacity than when he went in, but it looked like Cherry could hold it as well as Clint could.

"So you control the town as long as you control your men," Clint said.

"Oh, I'll control them."

"How do you think they feel now that they've seen you kill one of them?"

"As long as there's that bank to be had they'll do what I say."

"What happens if a bunch of them get together and decides to take the bank for themselves?"

Cherry studied Clint, running his hand over his jaw.

"That's a possibility," Clint said.

"Yeah, it might be. What do you suggest?"

"You'd better decide which men you can trust, and keep them near you and alert. You got any men like that?"

"I've got some," Cherry said. "Good ones. Dan Malone, Frank Carter—"

"I've heard of them," Clint said, "but their best days are behind them, aren't they? Have you got anybody else?"

"I've got an animal called the Breed," Cherry said. "Broke some bones that first day we were here."

"You control him?"

"As much as anyone does, I guess."

"I haven't seen anyone like that."

"You'd know him if you saw him," Cherry said. "Big and ugly as hell. I've got him watching the south end of town. Figure that'll keep him out of trouble."

"When do you let him out of his cage?"

"Late at night, when there's no chance of him running into anybody else. He comes in here and eats some, and then turns in."

"Drink?"

"He doesn't touch it," Cherry said. "Not whiskey, not beer."

"What about the others?" Clint asked. "They all look about Sangster's age."

"They are."

"They reliable?"

"Mostly."

"Did he collect them?"

"Mostly," he said, again.

"You trust them?"

Cherry laughed shortly and said, "I trust me."

"You need somebody else to trust."

"Yeah, maybe," Cherry said, then looked at Clint and said, "You mean you?"

"Can you think of anybody better to watch your back?"

"What's in it for you?"

"I want your word."

"On what?"

"After you get the money you want from Rogers, you'll leave the town be."

Cherry laughed and said, "Oh, no. You don't get it, do you?"

"What?"

"There's plenty of money in that bank," Cherry explained. "If that was all I wanted I would've come into town and robbed the bank, and then got out. The money don't mean spit to me, Adams."

"Then what—"

"I want Sam Rogers to suffer," Cherry said. "I want him to watch the town he built burn to the ground, knowing he paid me and I did it anyway."

Clint thought a moment, then said, "All right, I'll still watch your back."

"In return for what?"

"The people," Clint said. "When you decide to burn the town, I want you to let the people go."

Cherry stared into his empty beer mug and then said, "I don't know about that, Adams." He thought a moment further and then said, "Let me sleep on it."

"Okay."

Cherry stood up and said, "We'll talk about it some more in the morning."

"I'll be here."

"Yeah," Cherry said with a laugh, "I know you will."

He started for the door, and then turned and said, "Adams."

"Yeah?"

"Were I you, I wouldn't be here when the Breed comes in. He's never in a very good mood."

Clint said, "I'll keep that in mind, Cherry. Thanks."

Cherry said, "Call me Will," and went out.

Clint left the saloon late and went across the street. He found himself a doorway and took residence in it. Luckily, the night was warm.

In fact, it was too warm. The summer heat had not let up at all since Clint left Labyrinth, and even sitting in the doorway he was sweating. Just when he was thinking about going back inside for another cold beer, he saw him.

He knew it was the Breed as soon as he saw him. A big, hulk of a man with black hair tied with a bandanna. Clint couldn't see his face, but he didn't have to. When he saw the man again, he'd know him.

Cherry had been right about one thing. He'd have known him when he saw him, anyway, without waiting to spot him now.

Clint left the doorway and walked to his hotel. During the walk he thought about what Sam Rogers had told him, and about what Will Cherry had told him.

Somehow, it was what Cherry said that had the ring of truth to it.

TWENTY-NINE

Clint waited until the saloon closed—he could see the door from his window, and saw the light go out. When he was sure it was closed, he left his room, found the hotel's rear door, and left that way. Staying off the main street, he made his way to the mayor's house, and tapped on the back door. He was admitted by Sunny Davis.

"Hello," she said, closing the door behind him. Either she or her father had been smart enough to leave the house in darkness.

"Is the sheriff here yet?" he asked.

"Not yet."

"How are you feeling?"

"I'm all right."

"It must have been terrible for you," Clint said, unsure of what you said to a girl who has been raped.

He saw her smile wanly in the dark as she said, "I wasn't a virgin, so it's not as if I'd never . . . done it before. It's just that when you're forced—"

"Sunny! Who's there?"

"It's Mr. Adams, Poppa."

"Oh, Adams," the mayor said, entering the room. "Rivkin's not here yet. What's this all about?"

"I thought we ought to get together and figure out some way to get this town back."

"Well, I'm for that—" Davis began, but they were interrupted by another tapping at the door.

Sunny Davis opened the door and let Sheriff Rivkin in.

"Adams," he said, nodding.

"Sheriff, I was just telling the mayor we ought to discuss some way of getting the town back from Cherry."

"That's fine with me," the lawman said.

"Let's sit right here," Clint said, indicating the kitchen table.

"Sunny, why don't you go back to bed," the mayor suggested.

"I'm staying, Poppa," she said, sitting down. "I have as much stake in this as anyone—and maybe more."

Davis looked as if he might argue, but then thought better of it.

There was enough moonlight coming in through the windows so that they could see each others' faces clearly.

"How many men do you think you can put together, Sheriff?" Clint asked.

"I have three deputies, and probably three or four more I can count on."

"That's about ten of us inside, and six outside."

"Six?" Davis asked. "That's all the men Sam Rogers could spare?"

"That's all he had who we wouldn't have to worry might shoot themselves in the foot, or each other," Clint said. "We need men who can hit what they're shooting at—if and when it comes to that."

"*If* it comes to that?" the sheriff asked. "How else do you figure to get the town back if we don't take it?"

"I talked to Cherry tonight," Clint said.

"Where?" Davis asked.

"In one of the saloons."

"Alone?"

"Yes, alone, except for the bartender."

"Hell, man, why didn't you just kill him!"

"That wouldn't have accomplished anything," Clint said. "There would still be thirty or so of his men in town."

"Without him they'd just leave."

"Let me tell you something, Mayor," Clint said. "Without Will Cherry to keep them in line those men would probably take this town apart, peel open your bank, and *then* leave."

"He's right, Mayor," Rivkin said. "At least Cherry keeps his men under control. Without him . . ."

"All right, all right, I see your point," the mayor finally said, relenting grudgingly. "So, you talked to him tonight. . . ."

"Right. He feels he's been wronged by Sam Rogers,

and he may be right. I think he can be reasoned with."

"Will Cherry?" Davis said incredulously. "The man is an animal."

"Not really."

"Look what he did to one of his own men and to his own woman!"

"Look what he did to the man who raped your daughter."

"He killed a woman!"

"But he'd never rape one," Clint said. "What does that tell you about the man?"

Davis couldn't answer, but Rivkin said, "He has a certain code of honor."

"Right. At this moment he's hell-bent for revenge against Rogers for some past score."

"What could a man like Rogers possibly have to do with a man like Cherry?" Davis asked.

It was Rivkin who answered.

"People change," Rivkin said. "We don't know who Sam Rogers was fifteen or twenty years ago."

"Exactly," Clint said.

"What are you proposing we do?"

"Well, I'd like to try and reason with Cherry, but if I can't, then I think we should be ready with some kind of a plan of action."

"All right," Davis said, "you know about these things. What should we do?"

Clint looked at Rivkin and said, "You're the sheriff."

"I'll give way to your experience, Adams," Rivkin assured him.

"All right then," Clint said, "listen up. . . ."

* * *

Alone in his hotel room Will Cherry was surprised at how isolated he felt from the rest of the town and the rest of his men. He hadn't talked to someone the way he talked to Clint Adams tonight since his first year in prison. He'd met an old convict there who had listened to his sad story, and then had taught him to survive in prison. The convict's name was Mike Stoker, and he'd been knifed in the back a year to the day that Cherry had been brought to Huntsville. Cherry had felt very lonely and alone that night, the way he felt now.

He supposed he might have handled the situation with Sangster and Nina differently, but at the time it had seemed the right thing to do. Later, when he saw the looks on the faces of his other men, he realized that he might have been wrong. Later still, after talking to Adams, he knew that the Gunsmith was right. Some of the men must have been having second thoughts about following him.

He was going to have to make sure he had men he could trust watching his back. He'd talk to Malone and Carter in the morning, and later to the Breed alone.

What he still had to sleep on was whether or not to trust Clint Adams.

That is, if he could sleep at all.

Rivkin was the first to leave and then Davis said he was tired and was turning in.

"You go ahead, Poppa," Sunny said. "I'll let Mr. Adams out."

"All right. Good-night, dear." He kissed his daughter's forehead and then looked at Clint. "I'm glad you're here, Adams," he said, and extended his hand.

"It'll work out, Mayor," Clint said, shaking the man's hand.

"I'm much more optimistic than I've been since those men came here."

After the mayor left Sunny Davis said, "I'm more optimistic too, Clint—can I call you Clint?"

"Of course."

"Would you do something for me before you leave, Clint?" she asked.

"What's that?"

"Would you hold me?"

Clint stared at her. He wasn't sure that this was the normal reaction for a woman who had recently been raped—but then rape was not a normal occurrence.

"I know it sounds like a strange request," she said, "but I need to feel . . . like a woman again. I was degraded this afternoon—even more so because that man—he made me feel things, in spite of myself, that I didn't want to feel . . . am I making any sense?"

"I think so," Clint said. He moved forward and took her into the circle of his arms. She was wearing a housedress, and a nightgown beneath it, neither of which was very thick. He could feel the heat and the contours of her lovely young body right through the garments.

She pressed her head against his chest and they stood that way for a while. A few minutes later she pulled her head back and looked up at him, lips parted. It would have been very easy for him to lean down and kiss her, but he didn't feel it was the thing to do—no matter how badly he wanted to do it. She was an extraordinarily lovely woman.

"Thank you," she said, stepping away from him.

"Will you be all right?"

"I'll be fine."

"This will all be over very soon."

"I know," she said, "I know."

She went to the door with him, let him out, and then closed it. He waited until he heard the lock click, and then made his way back to his hotel.

THIRTY

In the morning Clint went down to the dining room and had breakfast. Although he'd suspected as much, he hadn't known for sure that Cherry was staying in the hotel with him. The man might have taken over someone's house, or had been staying in a rooming house. It was only after Sangster and the girl—Nina, her name had been—had gone out Cherry's window that he knew for sure.

He figured a nice leisurely breakfast would enable Cherry to come down and find him, and then they could continue their discussion from the night before.

When his breakfast came he ordered a second pot of coffee, and told the waiter to bring a second cup.

Cherry had awakened early that morning and gone looking for Frank Carter and Dan Malone.

Carter and Malone had found a house not too far from the mayor's where a couple of handsome, middle-aged ladies lived, and had decided to take up residence there. Thinking about Sangster raping Sunny Davis, Cherry realized that it had never dawned on him that the two ladies would be doing anything with Carter and Malone that they didn't want to do.

He hoped he wasn't wrong.

As a matter of fact, forty-eight-year-old Edwina Chambers and fifty-two-year-old Martha Herbert were very pleased that two of Cherry's men had chosen them to live with—and to sleep with. There were so many pretty young women in town that the two women were at first flattered, and then grateful that Carter and Malone had chosen them.

The house had two bedrooms. Carter and Edwina slept in one, while Malone and Martha slept in the other.

Both were attractive women, not beautiful, but handsome. Edwina was tall with a once-proud bosom that had started to sag a bit and hips that were showing her age. Still, Carter found her very comfortable and undemanding.

Martha was sort of chubby, with fleshy breasts and buttocks, but Malone liked her that way. They were more sexually active than the other two, and on this particular morning Malone had Martha spread-eagled and was lapping away at her when the knock came at the door.

"Oooh, don't you dare leave me like this," Martha said breathlessly.

"Frank, get the door," Malone shouted.

In the other room, where Frank Carter and Edwina had been lying awake, hip to hip, listening to the noises Martha had been making, Carter got up and said to Edwina, "Old Dan's gonna work himself into a heart attack, you wait and see."

"If Martha doesn't have one first," Edwina said, laughing. She was perfectly satisfied that Carter never wanted to try anything new with her. They usually settled for the customary position, and then rolled over and went to sleep together.

When Carter opened the door and saw Cherry there, he said immediately, "I'll get Dan."

"So, what do you think?" Cherry asked.

He was standing outside the house with Malone and Carter, and had just given them a short version of what he and Clint Adams had discussed the night before.

"I think he's right, Will," Dan Malone said. "You need somebody reliable to watch your back."

"We're with you, Will, and we're reliable," Frank Carter said, "but we ain't the men we used to be, if you know what I mean."

"If I didn't know better, Will," Malone said, "I'd say prison was the best thing to happen to you. You're our age, but you're hungry, and that hunger has kept you as good as you ever was."

"So you think I ought to take him up on his offer, huh?" Cherry said.

"I can't think of anybody better to watch your

back," Malone said. "Can you?"

"No, I can't," Cherry said, "but while he's watching my back, I want you two to do something for me."

"What?"

"I want you to watch him!"

After leaving Malone and Carter, Will Cherry went to the south end of town and made his way to the roof of the Feed and Grain.

There he found the Breed. When he called out to the man, the half-breed turned and stared at him as if he had never seen him before. That was always the impression he got whenever the Breed looked at him. It had bothered him for a while, until he realized that the Breed looked at everyone like that.

He had a short talk with the Breed, the gist of which was that Cherry didn't trust his men anymore, and wanted the Breed to be ready at a moment's notice.

"To do what?" the Breed asked.

"Whatever I ask, Breed," Cherry said.

"You trust me?"

Cherry grinned and said, "No, but your share's just been doubled."

"I get twice as much as anyone else?" the Breed asked, wanting to get it straight.

"That's right."

"You are the boss, Mr. Cherry," the Breed said.

Staring into the Breed's cold black eyes, Cherry was certain that he was the boss only as long as it suited the Breed's purpose.

That was okay. They'd use each other . . . for a while.

After talking to Malone, Carter, and the Breed,

Cherry went to the hotel and found Clint Adams nursing a pot of coffee in the dining room. He had no way of knowing that it was Clint's third pot.

"Want some breakfast, Will?" Clint asked. He watched the man's reaction to his use of his first name, to see if Cherry remembered giving his permission.

"Just coffee," Cherry said, sitting down.

"Sleep all right?"

"Fine."

"Think over what we talked about?"

Cherry sipped the coffee and said, "God, that's strong."

"That's the way coffee's supposed to be."

"Men, too," Cherry said. "Yeah, I thought over what we talked about, and I've decided to take you on."

"Just to watch your back," Clint said, reminding Cherry. "I don't have anything to do with what's going on between you and Rogers, or with you and the town."

"Just to watch my back."

"All right, then," Clint said, raising his coffee cup.

Cherry raised his cup and said, "All right."

THIRTY-ONE

Five men were gathered at a boardinghouse in the center of town. All five men worked for Will Cherry. They were all Johnny Sangster's age and had all been recruited by Sangster.

"You might have a point," one of them said to Cliff Norbert, the man who was doing all the talking. "If he'd kill Sangster, his right-hand man, he'd kill any one of us."

"I told you," Norbert said, "it's time to hit the bank in this town and light out. Are you men with me?"

"How many others?" someone asked.

"Just the five of us," Norbert said, "and one other man."

"Who?"

"Hank Wood."

"That old drunk?"

"Why do we need him?"

Norbert smiled and said, "You'll see."

Hank Wood sat in the livery with a bottle of whiskey, a bottle that Cliff Norbert have given him.

Norbert was one of the young men Cherry had hired, because he knew he couldn't count on somebody like Hank Wood. Young and smooth-faced, Norbert was one of those who laughed at Hank Wood, but the one who did the most laughing was Will Cherry. He treated Wood like dirt and laughed at him behind his back. Cliff Norbert said so.

Hank Wood had never liked Norbert, or any of the young men Cherry had hired, but Norbert had given Hank Wood a bottle of whiskey without making him grovel around in mud for it first.

Norbert had turned out to be a better friend then Will Cherry ever was.

Over a last cup of coffee Cherry told Clint that today was the day he was supposed to send a man to Rogers and tell him how much money he wanted for the town, and where to bring it.

"Who are you sending?"

"I *was* planning to send one of the young fellas," Cherry said, "but maybe I'll send Malone or Carter."

"Why not send the Breed?"

"Why him?"

"Because he'd intimidate Rogers, or anyone who

thought about starting anything. Can he handle a gun?"

"Almost as good as he handles a knife," Cherry said. "You might have a point." He looked at Clint and said, "After all, I can afford to send him now that I got you to watch my back, can't I?"

"If you say so, Will," Clint said. "Now we'd better get out of here before I float away on a river of coffee."

"Agreed. I'll send someone to find the Breed."

They stood up and left the dining room.

"Do you think Rogers will pay?" Clint asked.

"Not right away."

"How much time will you give him?"

Cherry grinned and said, "Enough for him to sweat off about twenty pounds."

They walked through the lobby and out the front door, onto the boardwalk.

"Just let me grab one of my men—"

"Will Cherry!"

Both Cherry and Clint turned to the sound of the voice.

"Is that Hank Wood?" Clint asked, staring at the filthy, emaciated drunk who was confronting them.

"It is," Cherry said. "You know him?"

"I did," Clint said. "Some years ago."

"Lookee here, Cherry, it's old Hank Wood, drunker than a skunk."

Cherry looked at Hank Wood and said, "He's drunk, all right. I told him what would happen the next time I saw him drunk."

"Leave him alone, Will," Clint said. "He's not worth it."

"If I let him go, the others will think—"

"You've got better things to do."

Cherry glared at Hank Wood, then relented and said, "You're right."

Cherry stepped off the boardwalk into the street, and suddenly Hank Wood pulled a gun from inside his filthy coat.

"Cherry!" Clint shouted. He pushed Will Cherry to the ground, drew, and fired at Hank Wood. His shot hit Wood in the chest, knocking him to the ground, where he died just seconds later.

Cherry picked himself up from the ground and said, "Looks like we agreed just in time, Clint. Thanks."

Cherry walked over to Hank Wood's body and picked up the gun.

"What made him do that?" Clint asked.

"He wouldn't have done it on his own," Cherry said. "He'd have to have been talked into it. This ain't even his gun."

"Looks like some of your boys have already made a move, Cherry," Clint said. "You may not be able to hold them together long enough to settle with Rogers."

"I'll hold them—"

There was a shot then, and before Clint could place it someone yelled, "They're robbing the bank!"

"You'll hold them, huh?" Clint said.

"I'll show them—" Will Cherry said, starting for the bank.

Clint started to follow, then heard a voice call out to him. It was Sheriff Rivkin.

"What's going on?"

"Get somebody on the roof to signal, like we planned," Clint said, "and then get some men to the bank. It's about to unravel.''

"Right."

Clint saw the mayor coming his way, but he had no time to talk to him. He was still supposed to be watching Will Cherry's back.

THIRTY-TWO

Cherry got to the bank just as four men were rushing out the door. A fifth man was in the street, holding the reins of five horses. He recognized one of the four men as a fella named Norbert.

All four men had their guns out, so Cherry drew his and shouted, "Norbert!"

Norbert turned and saw Cherry, and snapped off a shot at him.

As Cherry dropped into a crouch Clint came up behind him, gun drawn. As the four men started to fire at Cherry, Cherry and Clint fired back.

Two of them spun around and fell while Norbert and the fourth man reached the man holding the horses. The fifth man pulled his gun and began firing at Cherry and Clint, who dove for cover.

The three remaining bank robbers mounted up, but as Clint and Cherry fired, Sheriff Rivkin arrived, also firing. All three bank robbers fired back. A hail of bullets flew between them, and most of the lead found targets of meat and bone.

All three robbers were knocked from their horses by the force of the bullets. Sheriff Rivkin caught a bullet in the shoulder, and as Clint turned to look at Will Cherry, the man who had bottled up the town of Geneva, Texas, fell to the ground, bleeding from two holes in his chest.

Will Cherry died.

As Clint leaned over the body of Will Cherry, Rivkin said, "Here come the rest of his men, with the Breed right up front. They're gonna think we killed him."

"Maybe they'll decide it's not worth a fight when they see he's dead."

Clint stood up and looked toward Cherry's remaining men, who all had their guns out.

"Where are your men?"

"Up on the rooftops," Rivkin said, "but I don't think we have enough firepower—"

As Sheriff Rivkin said that, a group of men came riding down Main Street from the opposite direction, led by Joe Bowman.

Rivkin looked at Clint, who said, "Sam Rogers's men."

"Gonna be a firefight now," Rivkin said, wincing as the pain from his shoulder wound hit him.

"Maybe not," Clint said. "Let me see if I can talk to them."

"Adams—" Rivkin said, but Clint was moving toward Cherry's approaching men.

"Hold on!" Clint shouted, waving his arms. His gun was in his holster.

"Out of the way, Adams," an older man said.

"Are you Malone or Carter?"

The man hesitated, then said, "Malone."

"Well, Mr. Malone, your own men killed Cherry, not the sheriff, and not me."

"That's crazy—"

"They decided to take the bank themselves, Malone," Clint said. "Tell me none of you have thought the same thing since he killed Sangster."

The men exchanged glances, but none of them spoke up.

"Cherry's dead now, men," Clint said. "There's nobody to pay your way. Is that worth getting killed over?"

The man Clint was watching was the Breed. The two older men in front, Malone and Carter, would have a lot to do with what the men decided, but in the end they'd follow the Breed.

"What do you say, Breed?" Clint asked. "Want to take a chance on dying for free?"

He and the Breed matched stares for a few moments, and then the Breed shook his head.

"Not for free," he said. He broke off from the crowd and walked away.

That broke the logjam. One by one they peeled off and walked away. Some of them mounted horses right there and then and rode out of town; others would leave by the day's end.

Clint turned and walked over to where Bowman and his men were sitting astride their horses.

At the same time that the sheriff was waving his men off the rooftops Clint said, "It's okay, Joe. It's all over."

THIRTY-THREE

When Clint, Bowman, and the others rode up to Rogers's house, Sam Rogers and his daughter, Lynda, were waiting there. Rogers was frowning, but Lynda was smiling broadly.

Clint dismounted and handed Duke's reins over to one of the hands.

As he approached Rogers and Lynda, he only had eyes for Sam Rogers, to Lynda's disappointment.

"We have to talk," Clint said, and walked past him into the house.

By the time Rogers caught up to him he was in the man's office, waiting.

"What's the meaning of this?"

"Close the door."

Rogers turned and slammed the door.

"What happened?" he asked.

"Cherry is dead; his men are clearing out."

A look of relief came over Sam Rogers's face.

"Good job, Adams," he said finally. He walked behind his desk and said, "I'll get your money."

"Keep your money."

"What?"

"I don't want it."

Frowning, Rogers asked, "What do you want?"

"I want to know what you did to Will Cherry fifteen years ago."

"What are you talking about?"

"What happened fifteen years ago, when you and Cherry were to each rob a bank?"

"He told you that?"

"He did."

"And you believed him?"

"I did."

"You're crazy—"

Clint crossed the room and stood directly in front of Rogers's desk. Something on his face made Rogers lean backward, away from him.

"You set him up, didn't you?"

"I did no such—"

"You sent him into that town to rob a bank, and then tipped off the law so they'd be waiting for him."

Rogers pressed his lips tightly together, as if the truth were behind them, trying to get out.

"Yeah, you did. He ended up shooting an innocent bystander in a shoot-out and getting arrested. He got sent away for fifteen years, out of your way—only how was he in your way?"

"Your job is finished, Adams. Do you want to be paid or not?"

"Let me guess. The bank you hit had so much money in it that you didn't want to share it with him. You must have had some advance information about that, so you came up with the bold idea to hit two banks at the same time. Cherry goes to jail, and you get enough money to go straight and build . . . this . . . and Geneva."

"You can't prove any of this."

"I don't have to," Clint said. "I just wanted to know for my own benefit."

Clint turned and walked to the office door, and opened it. Lynda Rogers was on the other side. Apparently she was just about to knock.

"I'll tell you something else, Rogers," Clint said. "Cherry was killed stopping your bank from being robbed. *Your* bank, Rogers."

He turned and said to Lynda, "I'm sorry, Lynda. I have to go."

He left the house and went to the livery to get his horse. He mounted up and stopped to talk briefly to Joe Bowman.

Bowman listened, and then said, "What do you want me to do, Adams? I've got a good job."

"I know," Clint said. "I just thought you should know."

Clint rode off then, heading first for Geneva to see a lady, and then for Labyrinth, Texas.

He had a fee to collect, there.

EPILOGUE

Clint walked into Rick Hartman's saloon and approached the bar.

"Didn't expect you back so soon," T.C. said. "Beer?"

"Yeah," Clint said. He accepted the beer, then said, "Maybe you didn't expect me back at all?"

T.C. shrugged.

"I don't know where you went or why, Clint. You just always stay away longer than this."

"Yeah, I know," Clint said. "Where's Rick?"

"This early he's either in bed or in his office."

"I'll try his office," Clint said. "Give me a beer for him."

Clint walked to Rick's office door and knocked,

using the base of one of the beer mugs he was holding.

"Come in!" Rick called out.

Clint entered and saw Rick standing by an open window.

"Hotter than hell," Rick said, "and not a breeze to be found."

"Here."

Clint put the beer mug on the desk.

"Thanks," Rick said. "It's nice to see you back in one piece."

"It's nice to be back."

"How did it go?"

"Badly."

"Did you do the job?"

"Yup."

"So why badly?"

Clint told him.

Rick sat down and sipped his beer.

"That son of a bitch!" he said. "Sounds like Cherry had good cause."

"Not to burn down a town," Clint said, "but to expect some kind of revenge, yeah."

"And he won't get it."

"Yeah, he will."

"How?"

"When I stopped in Geneva to see Sunny Davis, I talked to the newspaper editor there."

"You gave the story to the newspaper?"

"Yes."

"But . . . it's the Geneva newspaper," Rick said. "Will they print it?"

"I think they will," Clint said. "Look what he made them go through. Yep, I think they will."

"I hope so," Rick said. "I'd like to see that bastard

get what's coming to him."

They both nursed their beers for a few minutes, and then Rick said, "Thanks, Clint."

"For what?"

"For clearing my conscience, and for fixing it so that I no longer owe Sam Rogers anything."

"You're welcome."

After a few more awkward moments Rick said, "Now you want your fee, right?"

"Right."

"About my father, right?"

"Right."

Rick frowned and said, "It's not easy for me to talk about my father . . . but—"

"Yeah, well," Clint said, standing up, "then forget it."

"What?" Rick said, as Clint headed for the door.

"I said forget it," Clint said, looking at Rick from the door. "Feel free to ask me for a favor any time, Rick—at no cost."

Watch for

VENGEANCE TOWN

eighty-fourth in the exciting
Gunsmith series

coming in December!

J. R. ROBERTS

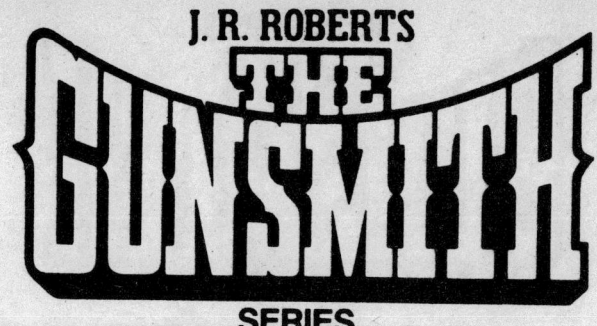

SERIES

☐ 0-441-30932-1	THE GUNSMITH #1:	MACKLIN'S WOMEN	$2.50
☐ 0-441-30930-5	THE GUNSMITH #7:	THE LONGHORN WAR	$2.50
☐ 0-441-30931-3	THE GUNSMITH #11:	ONE-HANDED GUN	$2.50
☐ 0-441-30905-4	THE GUNSMITH #15:	BANDIT GOLD	$2.50
☐ 0-441-30907-0	THE GUNSMITH #17:	SILVER WAR	$2.50
☐ 0-441-30949-6	THE GUNSMITH #45:	NAVAHO DEVIL	$2.50
☐ 0-441-30952-6	THE GUNSMITH #48:	ARCHER'S REVENGE	$2.50
☐ 0-441-30955-0	THE GUNSMITH #51:	DESERT HELL	$2.50
☐ 0-441-30956-9	THE GUNSMITH #52:	THE DIAMOND GUN	$2.50
☐ 0-441-30957-7	THE GUNSMITH #53:	DENVER DUO	$2.50
☐ 0-441-30958-5	THE GUNSMITH #54:	HELL ON WHEELS	$2.50
☐ 0-441-30959-3	THE GUNSMITH #55:	THE LEGEND MAKER	$2.50
☐ 0-441-30964-X	THE GUNSMITH #60:	GERONIMO'S TRAIL	$2.50

Please send the titles I've checked above. Mail orders to:

BERKLEY PUBLISHING GROUP
390 Murray Hill Pkwy., Dept. B
East Rutherford, NJ 07073

NAME_____
ADDRESS_____
CITY_____
STATE_____ZIP_____

Please allow 6 weeks for delivery.
Prices are subject to change without notice.

POSTAGE & HANDLING:
$1.00 for one book, $.25 for each additional. Do not exceed $3.50.

BOOK TOTAL	$_____
SHIPPING & HANDLING	$_____
APPLICABLE SALES TAX (CA, NJ, NY, PA)	$_____
TOTAL AMOUNT DUE	$_____
PAYABLE IN US FUNDS. (No cash orders accepted)	

A1/a

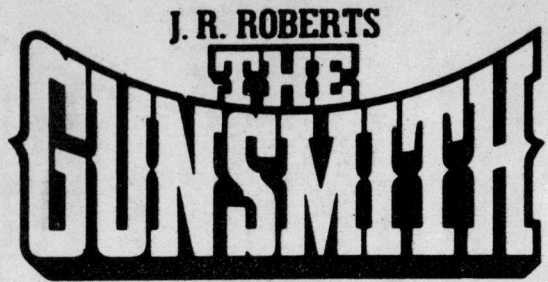

SERIES

☐ 0-441-30965-8	THE GUNSMITH #61: THE COMSTOCK GOLD FRAUD	$2.50
☐ 0-441-30966-6	THE GUNSMITH #62: BOOM TOWN KILLER	$2.50
☐ 0-441-30967-4	THE GUNSMITH #63: TEXAS TRACKDOWN	$2.50
☐ 0-441-30968-2	THE GUNSMITH #64: THE FAST DRAW LEAGUE	$2.50
☐ 0-441-30969-0	THE GUNSMITH #65: SHOWDOWN IN RIO MALO	$2.50
☐ 0-441-30970-4	THE GUNSMITH #66: OUTLAW TRAIL	$2.75
☐ 0-515-09058-1	THE GUNSMITH #67: HOMESTEADER GUNS	$2.75
☐ 0-515-09118-9	THE GUNSMITH #68: FIVE CARD DEATH	$2.75
☐ 0-515-09176-6	THE GUNSMITH #69: TRAIL DRIVE TO MONTANA	$2.75
☐ 0-515-09217-7	THE GUNSMITH #71: THE OLD WHISTLER GANG	$2.75
☐ 0-515-09329-7	THE GUNSMITH #72: DAUGHTER OF GOLD	$2.75
☐ 0-515-09380-7	THE GUNSMITH #73: APACHE GOLD	$2.75
☐ 0-515-09447-1	THE GUNSMITH #74: PLAINS MURDER	$2.75
☐ 0-515-09493-5	THE GUNSMITH #75: DEADLY MEMORIES	$2.75
☐ 0-515-09523-0	THE GUNSMITH #76: THE NEVADA TIMBER WAR	$2.75
☐ 0-515-09550-8	THE GUNSMITH #77: NEW MEXICO SHOW DOWN	$2.75
☐ 0-515-09587-7	THE GUNSMITH #78: BARBED WIRE AND BULLETS	$2.95
☐ 0-515-09649-0	THE GUNSMITH #79: DEATH EXPRESS	$2.95
☐ 0-515-09685-7	THE GUNSMITH #80: WHEN LEGENDS DIE	$2.95
☐ 0-515-09709-8	THE GUNSMITH #81: SIX GUN JUSTICE	$2.95
☐ 0-515-09760-8	THE GUNSMITH #82: THE MUSTANG HUNTERS	$2.95

Please send the titles I've checked above. Mail orders to:

BERKLEY PUBLISHING GROUP
390 Murray Hill Pkwy., Dept. B
East Rutherford, NJ 07073

NAME_____

ADDRESS_____

CITY_____

STATE_____ ZIP_____

Please allow 6 weeks for delivery.
Prices are subject to change without notice.

POSTAGE & HANDLING:
$1.00 for one book, $.25 for each additional. Do not exceed $3.50.

BOOK TOTAL $_____

SHIPPING & HANDLING $_____

APPLICABLE SALES TAX $_____
(CA, NJ, NY, PA)

TOTAL AMOUNT DUE $_____
PAYABLE IN US FUNDS.
(No cash orders accepted.)